D1584927

## NO FLOWERS
## FOR THE GENERAL

A corpse a night was pretty good going, even by Mike Faraday's standards, especially as they turned up in 'the friendliest town in the world'. The laconic private eye was sent out on one of his toughest assignments. The life of General Diaz was threatened, and then three turned up from Cuba out of the past. With Stella on the other end of the phone, and Patti Morgan in his arms, Faraday was in his element, as events mounted to the goriest climax he could remember.

BASIL COPPER

# NO FLOWERS FOR THE GENERAL

*Complete and Unabridged*

## LINFORD
*Leicester*

First published in Great Britain

First Linford Edition
published 2000

British Library CIP Data

Copper, Basil, *1924* –
    No flowers for the general.—
    Large print ed.—
    Linford mystery library
    1. Detective and mystery stories
    2. Large type books
    I. Title
    823.9'14 [F]

ISBN 0–7089–5774–9

Published by
F. A. Thorpe (Publishing)
Anstey, Leicestershire

Set by Words & Graphics Ltd.
Anstey, Leicestershire
Printed and bound in Great Britain by
T. J. International Ltd., Padstow, Cornwall

This book is printed on acid-free paper

# 1

## Enter Dame Dora

I was driving north. It was a biting cold day in November and the flurries of rain which starred the windscreen looked like they might turn to snow before long. The Buick's bonnet had ice on the front of it which didn't help the heater's function any, and I was already regretting my mission. It was a ninety-mile drive to where I was going and the woman who had sent me hadn't exactly impressed me as a model of clear-eyed sanity.

Not that she was round the bend; but her eccentricity was noticeable and my throat still ached from the pressure of her knee. That sounded like a pretty funny sentence as I repeated it to myself and I laughed out loud before sobering down. I switched on the radio then; it helped on winter drives and I didn't want any passing patrolman wondering about a guy

1

who cracked jokes with himself.

The Buick had a disconcerting rumble somewhere in the chassis and I didn't put the pedal down too hard in case one of the tyres was acting up; there was little traffic on the turnpike but all the same I wasn't keen on taking a header into an oncoming car. Dance music mingled with static came through on the radio and made the monotony bearable. It was nearing dusk and the stark outlines of the winter trees on either side of the straight four-lane carriageway, made a spiky frieze for my thoughts as I drove.

There was a black shadow in my driving mirror and a brief blip of headlights; I pulled over to my nearside and the low-slung, black Bugatti went by in a crackle of exhausts. He blipped his lights again as a courtesy; the blue smoke from the exhausts looked already frozen in the cold air before it dispersed. He disappeared down the infinity of road in about nought seconds flat. I smiled to myself in the mirror; that would have been me once.

Not now. Not any more. Not with these

roads. Or with this car, come to that. I slowed down again, saw the lane behind was clear and helped myself to a cigarette. I lit it from the dash lighter and flared out the smoke with satisfaction; as I put the pack down in my pocket, my finger touched the soft bulk of the shoulder holster webbing. The Smith-Wesson cradled in it, was almost unnoticeable, the weight was spread so evenly.

Not that I was likely to need it. This wasn't specifically that sort of job but you never knew. I pulled over to the centre of the road; a few cars were travelling in the opposite direction, pretty fast, despite the conditions. One or two of them even had their sidelights on. The day was burning out in a smoky sunset beyond the jagged points of the hills; presently another light flared beneath the sunset and I swung off the turnpike, on across the hard shoulder and into the clean shaved parking lot at the side of the dinette.

The red neon lighting spelled out Dino's in the amber dusk. I tooled into the lot, killed the motor and finished my cigarette. I checked my baggage, made sure the car was locked and walked on over towards the main doors of the diner. The Bugatti was parked near the entrance. The driving seat was empty; I leaned down and looked at the licence sticker on the windshield. No reason really; just part of my job. Being just naturally curious helps too. The car was registered to a character called Nelson Holgren. His address was in L.A. I went on over to the door of the diner, pushed it open and went on in.

A TV set with a thirty-inch screen was fixed above one end of the long, plastic-topped counter; a blast of sound came out of it. On the screen flickering blue figures went through the motions of a girlie show. No-one took any notice of it. The man behind the bar nodded pleasantly. He had a long, dead face; shoulders that sloped narrowly like coat-hangers and a faded blue bow tie spotted with grease. His hands were clean though; I'll say that for him.

'What'll it be, mac?' he said in a voice in which years of hash-slinging hadn't entirely erased the human element. I ordered coffee, toast and orange juice. I went over into one of the booths at the corner of the room where I could watch the parking lot and the thin rain beading the windows. It looked colder than ever outside. But in here it was pretty warm and before I started on the food I took off the white, belted raincoat I was wearing and stashed it on the booth bench.

There were only about half a dozen people in the place this time of the afternoon and they were minding their own business. The nearest was a distinguished-looking, middle-aged man with white hair who might have passed for Otto Kruger on his night off. I figured he might be Mr Nelson Holgren — the owner of the Bugatti. I got outside the food, watched the rain and pondered the exciting life of a P.I.

So far it had been a pretty peculiar day. And it looked like being more curious before I hit the sack tonight. It started in the morning. It was around eleven a.m. Business was great. I leaned back with my heels in the usual rut on my broadtop and took an inventory of the cracks in the ceiling. This soon palled and I shifted my position and started an intensely absorbing game of noughts and crosses with myself.

Stella had gone out to do what she called shopping and my last cup of coffee had been at nine a.m. This brought up a crisis of interests; whether to hoist my can in the air and make for the partitioned-off alcove where we did the brewing-up or to break-out my track suit and do a steady trot round the block. The central-heating in our building should have gone out with the Taft Administration; some people said it had. Anyways, it had its on-days and its off-days. This was one of the latter and the temperature felt like it was only a degree or two over zero.

I was seriously debating whether to shut up shop for the day and leave a note for Stella but I was glad I didn't in the end. To break the monotony I walked around the room a bit, put the milk on to boil and amused myself by standing at the window looking down at the boulevard. It had come on to rain again and figures in slickers and long plastic boots shone phosphorescent through the downpour. I watched the ballet of umbrellas for perhaps five minutes or so and then went over and made my coffee. I cupped the warm beaker in my hands, inhaled the fresh grounds and sat down at my desk. It was just then that the phone rang.

'Faraday Investigations.'

'This is Dame Dora Shouthat,' said a woman's voice pompously.

'I don't know any Dumb Dora,' I said cautiously.

'Dame Dora,' the voice corrected me in tones like chipped ice.

'And I'm Kublai Khan on my days off,' I said, lowering my guard. It was all of six weeks from Christmas but maybe the funny boys were starting in early this year.

'I'll give you just fifteen seconds to sober up,' said the voice, 'and then I'll do my best to see your licence is withdrawn. I'm the President of the Olde Englishe Tweed Company.'

'What can I do for you, madam?' I said, changing my tone rapidly.

'If you're a detective agency start

7

detecting,' she said in a voice that would have made pickles taste like molasses. 'Be over here inside a quarter of an hour and I'll tell you how.'

I got over there fast.

★  ★  ★

But first I checked with Charlie Snagge. He was an old friend at the County Sheriff's Office who had often been useful. He was useful this time too. I expected him to scream when I mentioned Dame Dora's name but he only shifted the gum to the other side of his mouth. I could hear that clear from where I was sitting.

'She's all right,' he said after he swallowed two or three times.

'President of the L.A. Chamber of Commerce this year. What's she done? Passed out stewed at the Mogambo?'

He started snittering. He sounded like he thought it was funny. When I'd seen Dame Dora later I thought it was funny too. But I didn't laugh till then.

'Just checking,' I said. 'She sounded

like she lost a few ball bearings here and there.'

'She's English, ain't she?' he said. He had a point. I thanked him and hung up. Then I left a note for Stella and drove across town.

The Olde Englishe Tweed Company was on one of the big boulevards in the ritzier part of town. The entrance doors seemed to be made of eighteen carat gold. There were small, severe windows on either side of the entrance, carpeted with red velvet. There was nothing in the windows but a chunk of marble apiece and a yard or two of tweed draped over them. But the way they arranged it made it look like the cloth cost about fifty bucks a millimetre. By the time I got out I figured that price was somewhere about right.

A commissionaire with an epauletted coat and a fine line in fierce stares opened the door for me with a beautifully controlled manner just this side of insolence. Inside, the place was full of glass cases, dresses, bolts of cloth and wall-to-wall snobbery. The commission-aire jerked a white-gloved thumb when I asked for Dame Dora; I felt like a third-class citizen before I had walked five yards.

I blipped the buzzer of the elevator and waited. Instead of a lift cage there was a box of polished pine which gave off the tang of varnish. Everything looked expensive. A girl in a Paris-cut suit looked at me mournfully from under her eyelids as she sagged gracefully against a counter. I didn't smile back. I felt like she might have charged me for it.

I went up three flights like the commissionaire had told me and got out in a corridor lined in natural wood; ceiling lights recessed flush with the wood gave off an even glow. The elevator wasn't manned, and after a moment the doors slid to by themselves and there was a whine as it went away. I went on down the corridor which was floored in mink, judging by the feel of it.

Typewriters were pecking from behind the doors and I could hear the chink of cups. I stopped at the end door of the corridor. It had stencilled on it in gold; Knock and Enter, so I did just that. It was quite a big lay-out. I fought my way across the carpet, which threatened to engulf me, to a railed-off area behind which were half a dozen desks. The walls were in quiet pastel shades and done up with big photographic blow-ups of Scottish scenery; where the tweed came from I supposed, though some of the shots looked more like whisky distilleries.

The typewriters stopped as I came through the door. There were about six girls, all young and nice-looking. The one nearest to me sat at a bigger desk than the others, which had three grey plastic telephones on it. She seemed to be in charge. She looked about twenty-eight; was tall and well-proportioned and wore a bell of gold hair about her face that looked as if it was real. She smiled, revealing seed-pearl teeth and put one of the phones back on its cradle.

'I'm Patti Morgan,' she said.

'That's nice,' I told her.

She smiled again. I noticed all the other girls were sitting watching us. It was a bit unnerving if you let that sort of thing throw you.

'You must be Mr Faraday,' she said.

'How did you guess?' I asked.

'She's already asked for you twice,' she said. 'I think you'd better go in.'

She jerked a well-manicured finger in the direction of a frosted glass panel set in the side wall of the office, just past the desk. She got up to open the gate set in the railing and held it wide for me. I caught her perfume as I brushed past. It smelled in keeping with the high tone of the rest of the place. The glass door had PRIVATE: PRESIDENT painted on it in gold on the frosted panel. I tapped on it and waited. The blonde job was on the phone behind me.

'Mr Faraday for you, Dame Dora.' She nodded and waved me forward. I pushed open the door and went in. I don't know what I expected but she had tweed written all over her. It was a big room and I couldn't pick her out at first. The whole place seemed to be heaped with yards of cloth; two big windows faced on to the street and the winter light spilled in and was lost in competition with the neon tubes. Then I remembered that they had to have good light for comparing shades of material.

Colour wash sketches of fashions were stacked on tables and around the walls; there were a few good pictures hanging here and there but they didn't make out too well with the competition from the other stuff. There was another big desk set down in the middle between the two windows. An electric fire in which imitation logs burned made a point of warm light in the wall that overlooked the boulevard.

Dame Dora Shouthat was a magnificent specimen when I got to see her. She had a pair of shoulders on her that made Carnera look like Toulouse-Lautrec. Her irongrey hair was drawn back in a bun from a face that would have stopped a Bronx bar-tender in his tracks. Her fingers stuck out in front of her like bundles of sausages at a pork butchers. Her breasts were like bollards that the Queen Mary could have tied up at. Amazonian wasn't in it.

In front of her was something that looked like a scale model of Vimy Ridge. I found out later it was her hat. It sported a pin as big as a knitting needle. I bet she used a baseball bat for a cocktail stick. The rest of her was mercifully hidden behind the desk. She was studying a jazzy lay-out some dreamy artist had cooked up, depicting females with sixteen-inch waists and forty-five-inch busts, dressed in a few square millimetres of chiffon.

'Planning to take up modelling?' I asked with what I hoped was a roguish leer.

'Don't be impertinent, young man,' she boomed. I regretted my foolhardiness. I guess bell-tents were more in her line. She regarded me sceptically and waved a pencil as big as an umbrella.

'Sit down and keep quiet for a moment,' she said.

I dropped into a padded chair and put my feet down among piles of fashion magazines that littered the floor. Seen close up Dame Dora seemed even more alarming. To make matters worse my chair was lower than hers. I felt like Gulliver. In Brobdingnag of course.

She put down the lay-out at last and

studied me. Fullface, if you could forget the rest, she had steady brown eyes that were full of humour. A smile was fighting to get out at the corner of her mouth.

'Identification?'

I passed her the copy of my licence in the cellophane window of my billfold. She studied it for a moment and then handed it back. She seemed satisfied.

'I hear you're in a discreet line of business, Mr Faraday, and can be trusted.'

I didn't contradict her. She frowned momentarily and ferreted about on the desk. Presently she came up with a powerful-looking black cheroot. She lit it with a chromium-plated lighter shaped like a knight in armour she took off the desk. It smelt like a cross between deadly nightshade and an opium-smoker's pad. She offered me one from a well-filled sandalwood box.

I shook my head. 'No thanks. I wouldn't want to be ill at the start of a case.'

She disappeared behind a pall of smoke and when she re-emerged she seemed to have made up her mind.

'Your fees, Mr Faraday?'

I told her. She hunted around among the junk on the desk and wrote on a slip of paper. She tossed the cheque across to me. 'There's a two hundred dollar retainer.'

'To do what?' I said.

'I want you to find this girl,' she said. 'She went missing two weeks ago.'

She handed me a slip of pasteboard. It was a photograph taken from her staff records. The upper half of the card was occupied by the photograph, the lower by typed statistics. The picture was a good, sharp one and showed a lively-looking girl of about twenty-five with fair hair trained back in a rather severe style over her ears. She wore a tailor-made suit and the smile on her face was natural. Her looks weren't exactly hard to take.

The record card told me all I wanted to know. Her name was Carmen Benson, the address was a private hotel for women only, over on the other side of town. The card said she was employed as a private secretary by the Olde Englishe Tweed

16

Company. I took the card and put it inside my wallet and put the whole thing in my jacket pocket.

'Anything wrong here at the office?' I said.

Dame Dora shook her massive head. 'Nothing like that,' she said. 'Carmen had been with me more than two years. We worked very closely together . . . '

I looked at her sharply but her face told me nothing. I wouldn't have said she was the sentimental type. Dame Dora blew acrid smoke out of her nostrils and disappeared from view again. When she came into focus once more, she went on, 'Something's badly wrong. She left L.A. to spend the week-end with her people as usual. That was on the Friday night. She never showed up on the Monday and we haven't seen her since.'

I took the liberty of lighting a cigarette. I was searching around with the spent match in my hand when she passed over an ashtray as big as a trash-can lid.

'You checked with her parents and the hotel, I take it?' I said.

'Of course,' she snapped. 'She arrived

home as usual on Friday. The last they saw of her was on Saturday evening when she went out to meet a boy friend.'

'The local police checked?' I said.

Dame Dora sighed, like she was talking to a child.

'That's why I'm hiring you,' she said. 'I want to know what happened and where she went . . . '

She hesitated a moment and a dark shadow crossed her face.

'And if she's still alive,' I finished for her.

To my surprise she screwed up her mouth like she was going to cry, but maybe it was only indigestion. Then she clamped on the shaft of the cheroot and went on pouring out smoke.

'Precisely,' she said. 'Here's the address.'

She passed me over another sheet of paper with some typing on it.

'Where the hell's Mudville?' I said.

'About 100 miles north of here,' she said. 'Just a small town. You'll want a large-scale map.'

'I got one in my car,' I said. 'Don't

bother. I'll check later.'

She nodded, studying me from under half-closed eyelids. 'I suppose you are the man to handle it,' she said more to herself than to me. 'You look usefully built.'

She stood up. I felt a little nervous but tried not to show it.

'Turn around,' she said. 'Let's see what you're made of.' She frowned again. 'You look all right,' she said slowly and shook her head.

She moved with unexpected swiftness and then the sky fell on me. I cart-wheeled over the desk and a knee that felt like an elephant's shinbone was rammed at my throat, pinning me helplessly. I rolled my eyes and tried to look like I was enjoying it. Just then the door opened and the blonde number came in. She had a job to control her face. Dame Dora took the hambone away eventually and I breathed again.

I fell into my armchair. 'Let that be a lesson to you,' I said when I got back my breath. 'I was afraid of breaking your leg, otherwise I should have put a reverse lock on.'

The blonde number turned red in the face, looked like she was going to choke and had to go out. Dame Dora considered me seriously. She stood up again suddenly.

'Best out of three throws?' she said brightly. I cracked then and it was her turn to burst into laughter.

'You'll do,' she hooted. 'You're as brass-faced as they come.'

★  ★  ★

When I got outside there was a strange quiet. All the girls were looking at me. The rustling of paper sounded like an explosion in the silence. Patti Morgan dabbed at her face with a screwed-up handkerchief. Someone had a fit of coughing at the back of the office. I went towards the door like I was walking on raw egg yolks. I felt twelve eyes burning into the back of my neck.

'In case you want anything, Mr Faraday,' said a voice at my elbow. Patti Morgan stood at the railing, holding the gate open. She was still fighting for control of her face. She put a piece of pasteboard in my hand. Later I found it gave a Laurel Canyon address and her telephone number. Right now all I wanted was out. I made the mistake of trying the casual exit.

'I was only humouring the old lady,' I said. 'I didn't want to hurt her.'

I took one look at their faces and went out the door. Even through the panels I could hear the roar of laughter from six throats. It almost lifted the roof. I mopped my brow and rode down in the elevator. I got in my car and drove away as quickly and quietly as possible.

# 2

## Careless Driver

When I got to the office building I parked the car in the usual garage around the corner and studied the card Patti Morgan had given me. It had written across the top; I'm free any evening.

I grinned and tucked it in my pocket. The wind came off the street like it had needles of ice in it. I rode up in the creaking elevator. It wasn't much warmer indoors. The waiting room was empty as usual. I went on into the main office. Stella sat at my desk powdering her nose. I'd never yet caught her working but the pile of typed letters in the tray belied her casual appearance. She went briskly over to the alcove with a clatter of high heels. I heard the click as she switched the small electric stove on.

I sat down at the desk, signed a few pieces of paper and reached for a cigarette. There was a thin rasp of a match and Stella lit it over my shoulder. She came and stood close behind me, put white arms around my neck and fooled with my hair. I stood it for perhaps half a minute and then I reached around in back for her but she was too quick for me. She skipped away laughing.

'What you want is coffee, to calm your nerves,' she said. I knew what I had in mind right then and it certainly wasn't coffee. Stella's figure and her honey-blonde hair had been featuring in my dreams for quite some while now, but she had her mind set on marriage and marriage and me don't mix. She stood fussing with cups and saucers and I admired the perfection of legs encased in light sheers, until she shifted round to face me.

I gave up then, signed the last of the letters and cleared my desk. She put down the coffee in front of me, slewed round the metal swivel chair from her own desk and sat facing me. Her eyes studied my face. I smoked on for a bit. Then I stubbed out the cigarette and drank the coffee. It tasted good, like always when Stella made it.

'We got ourselves a case,' I told her.

She took notes as I filled her in on the details. She frowned as I finished, tapped her teeth with the pencil. She picked up her coffee cup again.

'This Dame Dora sounds like a character,' she said. 'You sure I got the whole story, Mike?'

I hadn't told it like it happened, of course; that was giving a girl like Stella far too much scope.

'We swapped punches,' I said. 'I'll do better in the return match.'

'Sounds like she could handle the case all by herself,' said Stella mildly. 'What did she hire you for?'

'I get to hold the prize-money,' I said.

Stella's face looked great when she smiled.

'I'd better get you packed,' she said. 'We could drop out at your place after I finish off here.'

'I got that all fixed,' I said hastily. 'I'm leaving right away. I'll throw a few things in a bag on my way across town.'

24

She got up quickly and went over to the alcove. She fussed about with the cups rather too emphatically. I sat and felt a bit of a heel. It wasn't that I minded Stella packing for me. It was just that she was too damned attractive and my place too convenient. I should never have made it out of there this afternoon and I had to get moving. Stella came back and put down the second cup in front of me. Her hand rested on mine for just an extra fraction of a second. It felt dry and warm.

'Sorry, sweetie,' I said. 'But I haven't much time.'

She kissed me very quickly, on the forehead and then went and sat down. The kiss spread out and the warmth with it all over my body. Her eyes looked real bright as I drank the second cup.

'I'll go look up Mudville for you,' she said. 'Do you want me to book a hotel?'

I shook my head. I finished off the coffee in the second cup but still I sat on. Stella was busy with papers and large-scale maps.

'You leave town by the freeway,' she

said. 'That way you avoid the mountains in the dark.'

'Thanks,' I said.

'Sounds like a real one-horse town,' she said.

'I got news for you,' I said. 'They got two horses now.'

'Look after yourself, Mike,' she said. She was smiling.

'Sure,' I said. 'Ring in tomorrow.'

We kissed again before I left. Properly this time. I felt it all the way to Mudville. I gassed up the Buick at the garage round the corner and then drove on to my place. I lived over on Park West in a small, rented house, one of an identical row of cottage-style places, each with manicured lawns front and back, separated by low, identical hedges. I threw a few things into a grip, broke out the Smith-Wesson from the small armoury-cupboard in my bedroom, locked up the place and left town.

I drove out the way Stella said. She's always right and I knew if she said it was the best way that would be it. I had the large-scale map pinned to the dash where

I could see it; the going wouldn't get tricky until after Johnstown, the nearest sizeable place. After the turnpike beyond the town, it was about another thirty-mile drive over twisting, second class roads, until you came to Mudville, one of a string of scattered communities in that neck of the woods.

I turned on to the freeway and started to put miles behind me. The sky was already darkening when I last saw the lights of L.A.

★    ★    ★

It was almost completely dark outside Dino's and I could no longer see the outlines of the parked cars until someone threw a switch and the heavy duty lamps dotted about the parking lot burned a hole in the gloom. The rain made solid swathes between the windows and the hurrying cars on the turnpike beyond, whose headlamp beams pushed aside the darkness and the rain with fretful fingers. The music from the TV set had stopped and the dancing girls had

27

disappeared. In their place was some sort of panel game. The effect was, if anything, slightly worse. I drank the last of my coffee and lit a cigarette. Otto Kruger settled his check, got up and went out. He nodded faintly in my direction like he knew me. A short while afterwards there was a throaty snarl and the long, low-slung bulk of the Bugatti went down the parking lot, eased on to the turnpike and made off in great style.

As an entertainment it didn't rate very high so I paid my check and left. I had to sprint to the car and the rain had already penetrated the collar of my coat when I got the door open. The hood was getting worn and rain had begun to drift into the driving seat. I sponged it off and got behind the wheel. Dino's was a pink blur behind the curtain of rain as I eased up on to the road shoulder. I started making distance towards Johnstown.

It was fairly quiet on the turnpike now. I turned on the radio again and the saccharine melodies of the dance music helped to deaden the slurring of the tyres in the wet and the drumming of the rain against the windscreen and the hood. It was a solid wall of water out here, and the wind, which was rising, buffeted the car so that I could feel the tyres fighting the thick film of water on the road. I turned up the dashboard lights and cast a quick glance at the vibrating surface of the map. I had quite a way to go yet. I turned down the light again until the dials were dim circlets in the darkness and concentrated on the road. I huddled deeper into my raincoat and slashed on through the dark.

It was around seven and there was no moon so I knew when the lights of Johnstown started coming up. It was raining like fun but there was nothing else on the road; I guess most other drivers were being cautious like me. Except for Otto Kruger. He would be halfway across the country by now, judging by the speed he was making when he left the roadside diner. Two cars drifted towards me as I neared the outskirts of Johnstown; they were going dangerously fast and one of them had a yellow foglight on which made an opaque glare of my windscreen until he had gone past. Both cars were planing on the surface of the water-logged road, sheets of muddy spray sluicing off their tyres.

I turned on into the centre of town at a big T-junction where the lights of a roadhouse gave a momentary impression of cheerfulness. The shapes of parked cars looked like subterranean creatures in the aquarium-shape of my side windows. A big sign came up on my nearside; DANGER — DRIVE SLOWLY THROUGH JOHNSTOWN. I obliged by ghosting down to twenty. The wind was still buffeting the sides of the car, though it was sheltered here; a few lighted windows went by in the dusk.

A TV rental service, the brilliant explosion of a drugstore with the silhouettes of youngsters at a soda counter; the town's one or two big stores, a few hardy, middle-aged couples agape in the blank vacuity of their arcades; a patch of darkness; the shimmer of street-lamps. Then the well-barbered lawns of the residential section; more stores and shops, two or three biggish hotels with neon signs; a blue neon which spelt out SPINETTI'S; a side street of shuttered shops; the lights of a railroad depot; something that looked like a school with lighted windows.

The town frayed out into a few quieter streets, the Buick rumbled over a light railway line which crossed the road and then I was out on the last of the turnpike. At least the last so far as I was concerned. I glanced in the mirror, saw the lane was clear and eased over to the right, where a side road split off the main artery. There was a signpost but it was so faded I couldn't make out what it said as my headlamps chopped across it. But Stella had marked the map and this was the first turning after Johnstown, so it had to be right. The surface was pretty good and the road wide so I kept on going.

I lit a cigarette and inhaled the smoke gratefully. I shouldn't be sorry to hit the sack tonight. All I wanted was a decent flop and a grill room where I could get outside a good steak. The rest could take care of itself. Presently I passed the lights of a small place off among the trees and soon after I came to a cross-roads. The rain was slackening a bit now and I got out and had a look at the signpost.

The finger pointed off to the west. It said; MUDVILLE 15. I got back in the driving seat and tooled the Buick over on to the secondary road. This had only a dirt and grit surface and the rain had softened it so that the going was pretty tough. I stayed in a low gear and resigned myself to grinding on. The road wound upwards into the darkness; the headlights picked out drenched bushes fringing the track and the darker outlines of trees.

I kept on climbing in low gear; I was on a shelf among shallow hills. The gradient was nothing to speak of but the conditions made the going difficult. If I had a blowout here it would be a bleak prospect. There were small stones and rocky outcrops underneath and now and again streams of water from farther up the hill poured across in front of me. I looked at my watch in the dim light from the dash panel. It was half an hour since I hit the side road.

I figured I was about five miles away

from Mudville if I was on the right road still. Now there was a name. A rumble sounded as the Buick's front wheels ran over some projection. I slackened speed and soon a clearing came up. Lights were festooned from cables strung among the trees and a big concrete apron ran from the road.

Cedarwood cabins with lights in the windows were scattered about and half a dozen cars stood in front of a long, low building with steamed-over windows. At the back of a lawn strewn with the sodden leaves of winter was an illuminated board with the legend; Pinetop Motel. Restaurant-Bar. Abel Grunwohl Prop. I stopped the car and looked at the sign thoughtfully. The thin rain drumming on the car-hood and the part of the sign which said Restaurant-Bar clinched it. I put in the gear and rolled gently into the lot.

There was a wooden arrow on a tree with a lamp hanging over the top of it. It pointed away down past the restaurant area. It said; RECEPTION. I drove on along the narrow concrete ribbon of road and stopped in a parking lot in front of a small timber building surrounded by more sodden lawn. This had a white board hanging on chains over the door. This was lit too, with neon tubing. It said; OFFICE. Their electricity bill must have been something.

I switched off, got out of the car and drifted up the path and through the office door. There was a bare wood counter inside, a fly-blown calendar or two pinned on the thin composition walls. A plump man of about fifty sat behind the counter with his buttocks squeezed into a padded chair and sunned himself under a parchment shaded lamp. His interest in the racing page of his paper wasn't diminished by my presence.

'Mr Grunwohl?' I said.

He changed gear on the gum in his mouth and said without looking up, 'That's what they christened me, son.'

'I'd like a room,' I said.

'Day or week?' he said. He shifted on the chair, lowered the paper fractionally and explored the gum with his tongue. He kept his gaze fixed on a corner of the counter. He had a form book there.

'Depends,' I said.

He grunted. He rummaged in a drawer, came up with a printed card. He shoved it over at me.

'There's the rates. By the day. In advance.'

He jingled some keys while I looked at the card. The rates were pretty steep for this time of year. I booked in for three days. I paid him. He grunted again. He shoved a register at me.

'Sign here. Cabin Seventeen.' He pushed over a big key with a brass number tag fixed to it with heavy wire. 'Bar shuts at one a.m. if you want a shot before turning in.'

I finished signing. He turned the register round and studied my name with an incurious eye. He glanced out of the front window, saw which way my car was facing. He jerked a plump thumb.

'Keep on driving, son. Third cabin on the left.' It was the first time he had looked at me.

'Thanks, Gabby,' I said. I went on out. I glanced back at the door. He was

35

already deep in his paper. I drove on down the concrete road like he said. The third cabin was set back in its own strip of green. I turned the Buick off; the head-lights picked up the number seventeen in white letters on a black ground, set on a metal tag stuck in the lawn. I drove up a concrete ramp in front of the garage doors. There was a metal handle hanging from a chain right by my driving door.

I pulled it and the garage door swung upwards on a counterpoise, with a hardly perceptible rumble. The garage light came on at the same time. I drove on in and killed the motor. The rain beat steadily on the roof. I left the garage door up. I hefted my grip from the passenger seat and got out of the car.

There was a heavy teak door in the back side wall of the garage. It had seventeen painted on it in big white letters. The key fitted. I opened the door. There was a light switch just inside. It was a nice lay-out; natural pine walls varnished over; sporting prints; new contemporary furniture. The central heating was on. There were big picture windows in front, flowers in a metal vase, a green Swedish telephone on a side table. The door locked automatically behind me. I snubbed the catch.

I looked through into the room adjoining. That was done up in the same style, except that it was a bedroom. There was a large double bed set down in the middle against one wall, all-floor grey carpeting, another telephone on the bedside table and a radio. Beyond that was a microscopic hall leading to a front door giving on to a porch. Across the hall was a bathroom and shower. There were clean towels in the bathroom and the flat metal radiators gave out a lot of warmth.

I decided that maybe the rate was worth it. I carried my bag into the bedroom, put down the key on the bedside table and took off my raincoat. I found some wooden pegs in the hall and hung it up. I smoked a cigarette while I ran the bath. It was around nine by now. Then I sat in the bath and sang to myself and forgot about the night and the rain and the job.

It wasn't yet ten, the rain had stopped and I was just finishing my second Scotch on the rocks. I annihilated the steak and salad, finished off with apple-pie, whipped cream and black coffee. I decided I liked it at Mr Grunwohl's Motel. I left the waiter enough money for his car-fare home and went over to the bar for a package of cigarettes.

'Which way's Mudville?' I asked the bar-tender as I came away. He grinned and pointed down beyond the chain of lights which showed through the window. 'About a mile and a half,' he said. 'You can't miss it. It's the only high-life we got around here.'

I thanked him and went on out. I walked back past Grunwohl's office, got my raincoat from my cabin, put it on and drove back out of the lot. The bar-tender hadn't exaggerated. After a few minutes on a tolerably smooth tarmac road I saw the lights of the main street.

There was a white board set at an angle to the road. I stopped the car to read it. It said in bold black letters; MUDVILLE. Population: 6,000. And underneath it: THE FRIENDLIEST TOWN IN THE WORLD. Whoever thought that up had a good sense of humour. Then I re-started the motor and drove on. It looked like the sort of town that went with Carmen Benson's face. But it was bigger than I thought. And I was wrong in one respect. There were two main streets, with cross alleys connecting them. Nobody moved on the sidewalks as I went through. It was Johnstown again on a smaller scale. I got through the place in about a minute flat which gives an idea of its size.

Even so there was a cinema and two biggish hotels. I figured I'd seen enough. I didn't want to spoil the place for next day. When I got out of town I came to a crossroads and reversed. When the lights of the town came up again, I tried the other street, just for the hell of it. It may or may not have been a good thing but it was certainly my style.

I was sneaking quietly along minding my own business when I spotted something that made me put the brake on. I stopped the Buick, turned around again and came back. A familiar black shape was parked about fifty yards up a road called Cherry Drive. There were large bungalows set back behind tall hedges and groves of dwarf trees. No lights showed in the houses. I stopped the car at the end of the road and walked up. No reason really, except that I'm naturally curious. The Bugatti was parked with its wheels up on the low sidewalk, opposite a thick hedge. It was one of those new, re-built jobs that are all the rage now. There were no houses for two hundred yards in either direction.

That was unusual in itself. Unless the driver had gone to one of the bungalows opposite. But another blank hedge faced the road on that side and the nearest house entrances were farther down. I went round to the front of the Bugatti. There couldn't be two like it in the same neighbourhood. I felt the front of the radiator. Heat was still coming out of the grille. When I walked back along the nearside I saw the figure sitting in it. I was about to speak when I felt the old familiar sensation begin round about the base of my spine.

The driver was sitting jammed up against the door, his body unnaturally hunched. I got the door open quickly and a large, wet bundle fell against me. Something metallic and hooked tinkled down on the sidewalk. It was smeared and clotted with a substance that looked red even in the distant light of the street lamps.

Mr Nelson Holgren, if he was the licence holder named on the windscreen, hadn't died peacefully. Something had torn and hacked away the top of his skull. His silver hair was overlaid with carmine gouts and gashes and bone gleamed whitely. Scarlet ran out of his nose and mouth and caked on the front of his raincoat. His hands were spread out like claws on the steering wheel. He came out very slowly and gracefully from the Bugatti and hit the dirt.

# 3

## A Case for Sheriff Clark

I looked up and down the road. The scratching went away from my spine. Nothing moved except the shadows of the trees on the wet shine of the road. I couldn't lift the corpse back into the car without making a mess. But I carefully picked up the metal gadget, holding the end of it with the skirt of my raincoat. I wrapped it in my handkerchief. I intended to be away for only a short time but it might rain again any minute and it wouldn't do the finger-prints any good. If there were any.

Then I hot-footed it back to the main road. I had to get some law in pretty quickly before someone came along. And the person or persons who disliked Mr Holgren so much couldn't be far away. I turned around and drove quickly back into the more brightly lit part of town. I could see faint flecks of rain beginning to star the windscreen as I drove. I stopped at the first lit drug-store I came to. The small bald man behind the counter looked at me curiously. In the corner a group of youngsters in jeans and T-shirts gyrated round a shrieking jukebox.

He jerked his thumb vaguely out of the window. 'Go down two blocks the way you're facing. Tom Clark's office is in the square.'

I thanked him and went out. When I got to the place he said it was raining quite a spat; I was glad I'd kept the pick on the seat by my side. The square was quite a big one. It was lit by a cluster of white-globed lamps atop a fountain. The water was still going, even at this time of night. An oblong panel of light spelt out Sheriff's Office on one side.

I stopped opposite a carefully tended strip of lawn and went up a concrete path carrying my bundle. There was a round lamp of frosted glass over the front porch which cast a white radiance over the entrance steps. I went up the short flight. I went on in down a dim hall floored with linoleum speckled to look like black marble. The place was clean and well kept. The air smelt of warm soap and lysol.

There was a row of brown mahogany doors on one side of the corridor. A typewriter sounded from behind one of them. The third door on the right was the Sheriff's office. A thin sliver of light spilled from under it. I knocked once and walked in. It was a big office. A large man in a khaki shirt and well-pressed pants sat under an oak-cased wall clock and tickled the typewriter. I wasn't interested in him. Sheriff Clark sat behind an oak railing at a six by four desk that looked like it had some use, and fooled with some papers.

He was fairly tall, rangily built and had a tanned face that looked like you could trust it. He was smartly turned out as town sheriffs go in this neck of the woods. He wore a khaki shirt with a khaki tie to match under a shiny leather windcheater. It was unzipped nearly to the waist and his tin star gleamed dully on his shirt-front. It was the only distinctive thing about him; the rest of his appearance was neutral from his grey eyes to his pale brown pants and dark tan shoes. The butt of a revolver showed from a worn leather holster hooked over a Neanderthal hat-stand on one side of the room. He didn't look up as I came through the door.

'I'd be obliged if you'd shut it behind you,' he said mildly, turning over a sheet of paper. 'Kinda draughty this time of year.'

He reached out with one foot, hooked an old caneback chair, slid it across the railing and hefted it up to me.

'Rest up a little. I'll be right with you.'

I picked up the chair, set it down and lowered myself on to it. The man in the corner kept pounding the typewriter, an old-fashioned, round-bellied stove hissed to itself in a prim manner and the wall clock ticked on. I sat and studied a calendar advertising farm tractors, that was two years out of date. Clark finished fussing with the waste paper, pushed his chair back and took an old briar pipe out of his pocket. He studied me carefully as he filled it from an oilskin pouch.

'I can do something for you?'

I leaned over and pushed my licence across his desk. He flicked it with his finger and examined it warily. He closed his eyes and then pushed it back to me.

'We don't have any trouble in this town, Mr Faraday.'

'You got some now,' I told him. He went on filling his pipe. 'Meaning what?'

'Meaning that this isn't quite the friendly place you thought it was,' I said. 'Guy in a car up the street. Someone re-arranged his skull with an ice-pick.'

I put down my handkerchief on the desk in front of him and opened it up. The typing in my rear stopped abruptly. Clark paused in tamping his pipe with his thumb but otherwise my information seemed about as exciting to him like I had told him I didn't like coffee creams after dinner. Clark looked at the ice-pick as though he expected the killer's name to be stencilled on it.

'Know who the party was?' he said quietly.

'I'm a stranger here myself,' I said. 'Name on the wind-screen licence holder was Nelson Holgren if that means anything to you.'

Clark slowly lit his pipe with a match he struck on the corner of the desk. He screwed up his face like he was in pain as he drew on the stem.

'Could,' he said, 'but I'll ask the questions if you don't mind.'

'Suit yourself,' I said. 'I just thought you might be interested.'

He got up and went over to the hat-stand. He started buckling on the holster.

'Guess we'll go have a look-see,' he said. 'Stand by the office, Macklehenny.'

He adjusted the buckle of his belt and reached in the drawer of his desk. He re-wrapped the pick and put it away.

'What's your business here, Mr Faraday? Or are you just passing through?'

'I came up about the Benson girl,' I said.

He sighed. 'It figures. Guess we'll be seeing a lot of one another.'

He threw a bunch of keys at the back of his deputy. He didn't turn but a beefy hand stretched over his shoulder and plucked them out of the air. Then the typing resumed. We went out of the office and along the corridor.

'You got a car?' he said. I nodded.

'Then we'll take your heap,' he said. 'I have to justify my expenses if I cross the road for a soda. And the Town Council mightn't figure murder was important enough.'

We got in the Buick and I turned around in the square and headed back the way I came.

'Cherry Drive,' I said.

He grunted. His pipe made a small glow, lighting his face in the darkness of the car. The rain had started again and I switched on the wipers. I got to the Cherry Drive turning and stopped. I set the handbrake and we got out. Sheriff Clark turned up the collar of his windcheater and zipped it. He had a flashlight in one hand; I noticed his right rested on the butt of the gun. We walked lightly and easily round the turning, our footsteps covered by the thin sound of falling rain. The road was empty. I looked at my watch. I had been away precisely

twelve minutes. Long enough for someone though.

The Sheriff looked at me hard.

'You sure you got the right road . . . '
he began.

'It was here,' I said.

We walked on until I was opposite the
spot where I judged the Bugatti had been
stationed. The Sheriff left me and went
over the ground with his flashlight. The
sound of falling rain made a melancholy
noise on the leaves of the trees in the
darkness. He finished up and grunted
again. Then his revolver was suddenly out
and at my belly.

'You carry a gun, Mr Faraday?'

He put the torch on my face. His hand
came and expertly relieved me of the
Smith-Wesson. I buttoned up my raincoat
and we walked back to the end of the
road. He kept right behind me.

'We'll go talk this over at the office,' he
said.

'I don't blame you,' I said without
bitterness.

We got in the Buick and I drove back.

Sheriff Clark sat forward in his chair and put down the phone. 'You'd better run this pick into Johnstown first thing in the morning, Macklehenny,' he said. 'The lab's usually open by eight.'

I heard the deputy sigh behind me and then he started pounding the typewriter again. He hit it like he had a rock in each fist. The clock on the wall behind me said a little after midnight.

'I'd like my gun back if you don't mind,' I said for the third time in the last hour. Clark fingered the drawer where he'd placed it.

'You're not in the clear yet, Mr Faraday.'

'We've been through all that,' I said.

'All the same we had a nice quiet town here until you hit it,' he said.

'Have some sense,' I told him. 'If I wanted to beat somebody's brains out would I leave him by the side of the road, drive here to report it and bring in the murder weapon as well? Sounds likely, doesn't it?'

50

'Stranger things have happened,' said Macklehenny, in a muffled voice. It was the first time he had spoken. 'You get on with your reports, Charlie,' said Clark without heat. 'I'll do the thinking around here.'

He grinned suddenly. 'All right, Mr Faraday, I guess I was a little hard on you. I saw what was left of the bloodstains on the sidewalk before the rain washed them away. And there were tyre-marks leading off down Cherry Drive. Wouldn't have been no good following, because it's a through road which joins a main highway about a quarter of a mile on. I got a call out. We just got to sit tight until we find the car — or the corpse.'

'But you do know Holgren?' I said.

He nodded. 'Description fits someone I know. You planning to stay in town long?'

'Several days,' I said. 'I got my own problems. Benson girl was my assignment until I got side-tracked.'

He drew on his pipe, reached in the drawer and came up with my gun. He slid it across and I put it back in the holster under my armpit.

'You might start with the parents,' he said. 'Nice people. But I don't think you'll turn up much we haven't covered.'

'That's what I'm paid for,' I said. 'You want me to keep in touch with you?'

He smiled again. 'We'll keep in touch with you. Where you staying?'

I told him. He wrote it down on a pad. I got up to leave.

'Just one more thing,' he said. 'Keep this under your hat. No sense in stirring up the town unless we have to. We had enough problems before you blew in.'

'You act like he got himself killed just to impress me,' I said mildly.

Sheriff Clark shrugged. 'I had one disappearance to look out for when you showed up through that door,' he said. 'Now I got two.'

Macklehenny cleared his throat like he was going to say something. Sheriff Clark turned to look over my shoulder. Apparently Macklehenny thought twice about it. The typing started again. It was so loud I thought the machine was going to fall apart. Clark walked me down the corridor.

'You don't think the two things are connected?' I said. 'The Benson girl and Holgren?'

He shot me a long look. 'I hope to Christ not,' he said. He gave me a hard, dry hand to shake.

'I'm drifting around town tomorrow,' I said. 'I'll look in then.'

I went down the steps and into my car. It seemed like about two weeks since I left L.A. The rain had stopped and I didn't need the wipers.

I drove back to the motel. It was just after one when I sneaked into the parking lot. A few lights still burned in the bar and I could hear the clink of glasses as the barman washed up. There was only one car in the lot and that went away as I came along.

The rest of the place was in darkness. I drove in, lowered the door behind me and went on in to bed. I had a pretty good night, all things considered.

# 4

## The Seed Business

Next morning I drove back over to Mudville. As mornings go it wasn't up to much. The rain had been replaced by a needle-sharp wind. The gaunt pines and firs on the rocky outcrops of the surrounding hills were etched clear against the greyness of the sky and a solitary bird wheeled and dived above the tree-tops. I parked my car in the square near Clark's Office.

I pulled up the collar of my raincoat and walked a few blocks back to the drugstore I'd stopped at the night before. The town was a little more animated than it had been then. The same bald-headed man lounged behind the drugstore counter; it even looked like the same crowd round the juke-box. I bought a book of matches from a stand next the counter. While he got the change I asked him for the Benson place.

'Maple Street. They got a store,' he said. His eyes were alive with curiosity. 'You a friend of theirs?'

'I didn't say,' I said.

That didn't faze him. 'You walking?' he said. 'It's quite a step. The other end of town, the main street running parallel with this. They're in the seed business.'

I thanked him and left. When I got outside there was the honking of a horn behind me. A big blue and white car with a spotlight mounted in a bracket on the windscreen upright was parked outside the drugstore. It had a police sticker on the door panel. The side window was wound down and Sheriff Clark's head was sticking out of it. I couldn't make up my mind whether it was design or accident. Our meeting I mean, not his head.

'Nothing useable on that pick,' he said gloomily. 'Macklehenny just phoned in. Thanks for bringing it, though. Makes a nice paperweight.'

He started the engine and looked at me. 'Going somewhere?'

'Benson's,' I said.

I got in beside him. He tooled the car out cautiously into the traffic. He flipped a switch on the dashboard and a small red light went on and off. I figured it tied up with the red dome-light on the roof of the car. Whatever it was, the traffic gave way to him.

'Keeping tabs on me?' I asked.

He grinned. 'You got a suspicious mind, Mr Faraday. Just trying to be helpful.'

He swept the car round a corner and down the intersection into the parallel street. A big grey station wagon driven by a woman in a turban with a florid face to match hesitated and stalled in front. Clark swore, gave her a blast of the horn and pulled smoothly round, all in one movement. We missed the front of the station wagon by all of three inches.

'What you make of the Benson business?' I asked.

He hesitated a moment. 'I think the boy friend knows more than he's tellin'. I put the whole thing down to a false alarm at first. I figured she'd run off with someone and her parents were ashamed to talk. Now, I'm not so sure. She was pretty keen on this young fellow and he's still right here in town, which knocks that theory down.'

'You got his address?' I asked.

'I forgot,' he said blandly. 'Look me up some time at the office and I might remember it.'

He pulled in at the end of the parallel street, almost at the point where it started to run out of town. It was a large, new-painted store with the window full of green garden tools, rollers, hedge-trimmers and such-like. There was a neon sign over the top which said; JABEZ HARDWARE BENSON.

'Thanks, Sheriff,' I said and got out.

'Any time,' he said, leaning over to the window on my side of the car.

'You will keep in touch, won't you?' he said. 'I wouldn't want you to leave town without letting me know.'

'Sure,' I said.

He waved and pulled away from the kerb. I went on into the store. There were two or three people in the place admiring the coloured pictures on the seed packet advertisements. They seemed to start planning their gardens early in Mudville. I waited a few minutes and then a plump, well-fleshed man in a smart grey tussore suit with a dark tie came out from a cubby-hole office at the end of one counter. He had pince-nez clamped down over the bridge of his nose but despite the wide smile he didn't look too happy. I figured he must be Jabez Benson.

There was a small desk lit by a shaded lamp inside the office and a grey-haired woman in a green smock sat at the desk and operated an adding machine. She looked like she was doing the year's accounts for General Motors. The plump man blinked at me and put out his hand. He probably mistook me for a seed salesman.

'Mr. er . . . ' he said, like he was searching around inside his head for a name. He didn't come up with it.

'You wouldn't know me,' I said. 'You got somewhere private where we can talk?'

He seemed taken aback. 'You're not

from Cartarett and Spalding?'

'I'm sure they're very nice people but I'm afraid not,' I said.

'It's about your daughter.'

I had lowered my voice but quiet as it was in this corner of the store the grey-haired woman made a mess of her adding machine operations. I thought she was going to fall down. Benson didn't look too good either. He went yellow around the nostrils.

'It's not bad news, Mr Benson,' I said quickly. 'I'd just like to ask you a few questions.'

'Certainly,' he said hastily. 'Come inside. It's just that mother and I have been under rather a strain these last few weeks.'

We went into the glassed-in cubbyhole, brushing past his wife. 'Tell Perkins to take over, Emmy,' he said, 'and then come into the parlour. I'm sure this gentleman would like a cup of coffee.'

We squeezed through a tiny glass door in back and went on into a living room. It had a desk on one side which was cluttered with papers. Solid black leather armchairs were dotted about; there was a view of trees through a large window. Right now the place was pretty gloomy and the November light didn't show much detail. Benson must have been conscious of this because he went round switching on green-shaded lamps. He seemed to have a collection of them all over the room. They only succeeded in carving big chunks out of the shadows, the way shaded lamps always do. When he'd finished he stood rubbing his hands together like he was listening for something. His wife was suddenly back in the room.

'Do sit down, Mr . . . ,' she said, echoing her husband's earlier words.

'Faraday,' I said and eased myself into one of the big black chairs opposite an ornate teak coffee table. Mrs Benson looked at me curiously. She had a strong face, with a high, broad forehead and thick eyebrows.

'Are you a friend of my daughter, Mr Faraday?'

'By proxy, Mrs Benson,' I said. 'I don't know her personally.'

I got out one of my cards and gave it to Benson. He held it upside down for a minute, blinking painfully through his glasses at it. When he got it right way up he looked at it like it had about half an hour's worth of reading on it and then passed it to his wife. He licked his lips.

'A detective, eh . . . ' He made a helpless movement of his hands.

'I'm here to help your daughter,' I said. 'Her employer engaged me.'

I couldn't bring myself to say that ridiculous name. I could still see Dame Dora's features and feel the pressure of that gigantic knee. Mrs Benson moved in the dusk. She put the card down on the coffee table.

'She's a nice woman,' she said quietly. 'We'll help all we can.'

Benson coughed awkwardly and shifted over until he was sitting on the arm of the chair opposite me.

'It's a cold day, Emmy,' he said. 'Let's have some coffee and then perhaps we can tell Mr Faraday what he wants to know.'

61

I drank my third cup of coffee and dragged at my second cigarette. The room seemed full of warmth and smoke.

'This a good likeness?' I said. I got out the office record card Dame Dora had given me. I'd studied it often lately. It seemed to me now like a face Mudville wouldn't be seeing again. Mrs Benson clutched at the picture. Her eyes filled with water. Benson coughed embarrassedly. I looked in front of me and picked up my coffee cup again.

'A very good likeness, Mr Faraday,' the old lady said in a choked voice. 'We haven't seen this one, father. Perhaps we could get one from the company.'

'I'm sure you can, Mrs Benson,' I said. 'I'll mention it next time I go there. Right now I'd like to learn a little more about your daughter's background. Any objection to me having a look at her bedroom?'

Benson got up clumsily. 'Not at all,' he said. 'Though I don't think you'll find anything. The police went all over it very thoroughly.'

He led the way through the parlour into a wide hall. White-painted balustrades led up into a high-vaulted staircase. There were cut store-flowers in bowls on dark wood furniture. The whole effect was more elegant than the impression I got of the rest of the place. Benson started up the stairs and we followed.

'The last you saw of your daughter was about three that afternoon?' I said.

'That's right,' he answered over his shoulder. 'She was going out for tea and taking in a movie afterwards. We didn't start worrying until about eleven o'clock.'

'We thought she'd probably gone over to Patti Morgan's afterwards,' said Mrs Benson, as we went along a broad landing and fetched up in front of another white-painted door.

It didn't register for a moment. 'What did you say, Mrs Benson?' I asked.

'Patti Morgan,' she said. 'She's a girl works with Carmen at the Tweed company. She lives in Mudville too.'

The hell she does I thought to myself.

'Didn't you know?'

'No,' I said.

'Strange,' said Benson, opening the door and motioning me into a large bedroom with two windows facing south. 'I thought she would have mentioned it if you'd seen her yesterday.'

'There wasn't time,' I said.

'Oh, well,' Benson said, 'it makes no matter because Patti hadn't seen her, leastways not since they got off the L.A. train on Friday night.'

I nodded. I went round the apartment while the two of them stood helplessly in the middle of the room, by the big rosewood bed with its immaculate white coverlet. The room was the sort of place I should have expected a girl like Carmen Benson to have. Small town charm; chintzy curtains, quiet, tasteful wallpaper; a few books; surprisingly, Vanity Fair, Tender is the Night, Hemingway's Old Man and the Sea, Tobacco Road, some back copies of the New Yorker. A Vassar pennant on the blank space on the side where the bed met the wall.

There was a pink silk pyjama case standing at the bed-head. I examined a large silver-framed photograph standing on the bureau; it was a college group. Carmen was sitting in the second row. She had the same wistful, almost defiant look like she had in the picture in my pocket, the hair still drawn back from her face in that rather prim way. The Bensons started opening drawers and cupboards for me but I had seen enough.

I looked out of the window. There was nothing but dark trees, some pasture with an old horse grazing; then the wet strip of the main road and beyond that the low hills. It would have been a nice view in summer. We went downstairs again. We all three stood in a semi-circle in the parlour like we were waiting for someone.

'The Sheriff said something about your daughter having a boy friend in town,' I said. 'I wonder if you could give me his address.'

I was surprised by Benson's reaction. His face coloured up, he clenched his hands at his side and when he spoke, his voice came out with a rushing choke.

'The Sheriff had no right to say such things, Carmen had no boy friends in this place and anyone tells you different is a

65

liar. Now, if you'll excuse me, Mr Faraday, I've got business in the store.'

'Sure,' I said quickly, 'and thanks for your help. If I hear anything I'll let you know.'

He mumbled something, shook hands perfunctorily and went back into the office.

'I'll show you out the private way, Mr Faraday,' said Mrs Benson in an unnecessarily loud voice.

We went out into the hall. Mrs Benson opened a door which led on to a porch facing the street. She looked at me closely, like she was searching my face for an answer.

'There was a boy,' she said quickly, as she started to close the door. 'My husband didn't approve. You know how it is in small towns. He feels he's got something to do with Carmen's disappearance, though God knows, the police have questioned him enough. He works at the Redbarn Auto Showrooms a few blocks from here. Newton Cheney is his name.'

She grew thoughtful. 'Carmen could

have done worse for herself. He's a good-looking boy. But Jabez doesn't like car salesmen on principle. I'm afraid there were lots of rows between him and Carmen about it when she was home on week-ends.'

She sighed heavily and caught hold of my sleeve. She put her head up close to mine.

'You've got a strong face, Mr Faraday, and an honest one. Find my girl for me.'

'I'll try, Mrs Benson,' I said awkwardly. She shut the door quickly. I went out and latched the gate behind me. I went down the sidewalk feeling sorry I wasn't God.

★  ★  ★

The Redbarn Auto Showrooms was on one of the side roads between the two main streets. It stood next door to the Adair-House Hotel, which was pretty ritzy as small towns go. It was a two storey white box with a wide ramp at rear so that cars could be shown on two floors. There was nothing so vulgar as petrol pumps at the front; they were stacked away at the side. A discreet arrowed sign, white on blue, said GAS and pointed away from the showroom. There were blue lettered neons which gave all the classic names; FORD: CHEVROLET: CHRYSLER: DODGE: BUICK.

The ground floor was all glass. Up on the second floor cars revolved on turn-tables. They had big windows there too. You could walk up the ramp and along a small gallery outside to see these. The neons gave all the O.K. foreign names here; MERCEDES-BENZ; PEUGEOT: CITROEN: RENAULT: ROLLS-ROYCE: BENTLEY: SIMCA. I walked in through the massive plate-glass doors. A bell buzzed somewhere in the silence. There was thick grey carpeting; several gleaming new cars went round on their turn-tables. A big printed symbol, gold on blue said: WE ARE HERE TO SERVE YOU.

A large man in a blue pin-stripe suit and a pale green polka dot bow-tie swam in through the plate glass by a rear door. A pink-faced blonde secretary was smoothing down her dress. The big man sneered his way through the showroom towards me. He had mean, whisky eyes, receding black hair and something like a dead ferret under his nostrils. He was nearly up to me before I saw it was a mustache. He had face-powder on his shoulder too but he didn't notice that until after I'd gone out. That made him madder than ever.

'Can I help you sir?' He contrived to make the pleasantry offensive.

'I'd like to speak to Mr Newton Cheney,' I said.

'Who wants him?' he said, an edge coming into his voice.

'I do,' I told him. 'Is he here or isn't he?'

'No,' he said through his teeth.

'Thanks for the information,' I told him. 'I'll be back.'

'We close at four today,' he said to my shoulder blades, with what sounded like a grinding of incisors.

'You'll sell a lot of Frazer-Nashes with that technique,' I told him.

He did make an effort then to come towards the door, but it was too late.

'Don't rupture yourself,' I said. 'I'll

show myself out.' When I got outside I looked back. The big fellow was brushing face-powder off the front of his jacket and bawling out someone in the inner office. I grinned and went on down the street. Farther down I found a Post Office. I went into a booth and after a little trouble with my change, I dialled long distance. Stella sounded pretty good.

'We got ourselves some trouble,' I told her. 'A guy called Nelson Holgren got himself killed last night when I arrived.'

'My, we are on form,' she said drily. 'Is this connected with the Benson girl?'

'This is just a great town for murder,' I said. 'What I want you to do is to check the L.A. Directory and find out what you can about him. Give me a ring at the Pinetop Motel after nine tonight.'

I gave her the number.

'How did you make out with the Benson case?' she said.

'Too early to say,' I said. 'The Sheriff up here started in by arresting me but we're on the same side now.'

She chuckled. After I hung up I walked back down town. It did me good. The bald-headed man in the drugstore gave me a nod as I went by. At that distance it passed for friendly. When I got to my car there was a piece of folded paper tucked under one of the windscreen wipers. At first I thought it was a parking ticket but when I unfolded it, there was just one line on it, scribbled in thick pencil: Come On In.

I went down the hall to Sheriff Clark's office. It seemed busy today. All the other offices were occupied, of course, but there was still too much noise coming from his part of the building. I knocked and walked in. The room was full of people. There were at least half a dozen behind the oak railing, and others stood around outside. One or two were obvious pressmen and another seemed to be strung with cameras from head to foot. Macklehenny had a long-peaked baseball type of cap on his head and his revolver was buckled on. The typewriters were hooded. Somewhere in the back a radio was bleating.

As I came in Clark caught sight of me and put down the phone. 'You're just in time, Mr Faraday,' he said. 'We're waiting for the doc. They dragged that car of yours out of the river, about eight miles north of here. You want to go along?'

I nodded. 'I'd like that,' I said.

# 5

## Compost

I leaned against the bonnet of Sheriff Clark's patrol car and smoked. Way down the slope, where the cable thrummed taut against the rocks and thin winter grass, the Bugatti was being winched up through the dark brown water. Nothing of it was visible, but the streaks of white where the cable entered the water showed the strain. The cable ran to the winch of a bright red commercial operator's truck which was parked on the road above us.

Knots of people stood about the slope and murmured to themselves. At the top the road edge was lined with curious faces, thick as flies, and State troopers in black leather slickers kept them back. The Bugatti driver had been identified as Holgren. The body had already been removed by police frogmen and the doctor was at work behind a low canvas screen about a hundred yards from where we stood. Two lines of torn turf clear down to the water's edge showed where the sport job had gone over the night before.

The stream was called the Agano and it was pretty high right now. The current rode past at a fast lick and slewed the cable and its burden sideways. The police frogmen must have had a fair job of it. I looked down again to the muddy stream where November leaves and small branches were eddying past. Farther on, its course was lost among dark boulders and the darker stretches of the ragged winter trees; but below us there was a clear space without trees which ran along the bank for several hundred yards. It was the only possible place for some miles where the car could have gone over with any chance of getting to the water.

This argued fair local knowledge, some degree of nerve and a lot of confidence in the dark. There was only a white-painted plank fence at this point. As the road was narrow it looked like the car had no room to charge the fence. The killer had simply put the Bugatti broadside on across the road and butted the fence two or three times until the planks broke. Nerve, confidence and local knowledge again. The terrain was flat for a car's length just beyond the fence, then it dropped suddenly down the hillside. The killer would have joined Mr Holgren under water if he had misjudged his play.

'What's the word, Mr Faraday?'

A figure in an off-white trench coat had just appeared at my elbow. His brown snap-brim fedora had a card tucked into the band of it; his eyes were sharp; he wore a light mustache like a shaving brush and a collection of cameras strung round his shoulders. His dark grey trousers were tucked into rubber waders. I recognized him as a staff man on the *Examiner* back in L.A.

I filled him in on a few details while Clark kept a rather worried eye on me from a few yards down the slope.

'You'd better check out with the Sheriff,' I told him, just to keep Clark happy. 'Pass the stuff along to the wire boys, Harry,' I added. 'It might keep the locals off my neck a piece.'

He nodded and went off down the slope. I saw him tap Clark on the shoulder and then they went into a huddle. The Sheriff joined me a short while after.

'This lot must have gone over 'bout the time we was conferring last night,' he said drily. 'Seems to put you in the clear.'

'You telling me something or just thinking out loud?' I said.

He shrugged. 'No offence, Mr Faraday, but the town pays me to suspect everybody. Now you're off the hook. This makes it official.'

He looked moodily back down the slope. The rear of the Bugatti had broken water; I could read the red-numbered licence plate.

'The blood groups match,' said Clark. 'That ties in the ice-pick. We checked hotels and bars for a good distance around; nothing's been missed. It's a brand made clear across the nation. Could have been purchased anywhere. Doc says the operator got to work on Holgren from the rear seat. From the

76

angle of the first wound looks like he was talking to someone in the passenger seat when he got it.'

'That makes two men at least,' I said.

The Sheriff got out his old briar and put a match to the bowl. He screwed up his eyes as he drew in the smoke. He flipped his match down the slope.

'Or a woman,' he said.

The *Examiner* man came back with his cameras. He made me and Clark lean against the patrol car for pictures, then he took shots of the two of us separately. He went away pretty happy. I figured he had made around three thousand dollars in about seven minutes flat.

The car was up out of the stream now; water poured in white rivulets from the doors and windows. The noise of the winch ceased. Flash bulbs started popping down near the water's edge; there were police photographers as well as the agency boys.

'Seen enough or do you want to hang on here?' said Clark, looking at me.

'Not my case,' I said.

He went down the slope and conferred

with a small group of officers in black slickers. Then he re-joined me and we made our way up to the plank fence. The crowd was still clustered thickly along it and we had to elbow our way through. Clark did a bit of feet-stamping, judging by the row that accompanied his progress. We got into another police car. Clark drove two hundred yards down the road, turned around on a place where the verge was wider and went back the way he had come.

He had to use the siren when he got to where the crowd blocked the road; they didn't edge away until the wings of the car were almost touching the nearest moochers. Guess they didn't normally get so much excitement until the State Fair came around every five years. The Agano threaded its way, brown and oily through the trees. Clark switched off the siren and we rolled slowly down the steep road back to town. I could still see the Bugatti and the frozen groups around it, until a rising fold in the ground hid the scene from view. Then we hit tarmac and Clark started letting her out.

Clark dropped me back in the square when we got to town again. He leaned against the wheel and fished for his pipe.

'I'd like a proper statement from you, Mr Faraday, just as soon as we can get around to it.'

'Sure,' I said. I got back in my own car. I looked at my watch. It was after two and Redbarn Autos closed at four today according to the big guy who had been so lavish with the courtesy. I drove down a few blocks, found a place to park near the garage and looked for a lunch counter where I could make a quick exit without attracting too much attention.

The waitress in the pink gingham outfit with the white Dutch collar and cuffs was inclined to be chatty but the service was good and the food not entirely expendable. I settled myself into a corner booth facing the street and finished up with two helpings of apple pie and cream. I was on my second cup of coffee and the place was thinning out around three-thirty before I saw something which interested me.

A red Simca drove up to the front of the Redbarn Auto Showrooms. A young man with dark hair, dressed in a grey suit, got out, went into the main showroom and emerged again a couple of minutes later. He drove round to the pumps at the side of the building and gassed up the car. He didn't pay for the gas but signed a chit the attendant brought out; they chatted and joked together for a bit.

I settled up my check, left the lunch counter and got into my own car. I sat and smoked and kept an eye on Redbarn Autos. It was around a quarter past four before anything else happened. The same man in the grey suit came out from the main showroom and slammed the door behind him. He pushed it to make sure it was locked. I got ready to start the Buick but he didn't go back to his car. He crossed the boulevard obliquely in front of me. I got out quickly, slammed my door and followed.

I didn't have far to go. He walked easily, perhaps two blocks and stopped in front of a double-window beauty shop, all chrome and guilt. He went through a small side door. I followed and stopped almost opposite. I studied my paper while my eyes gave the door the once-over. There was a box sign set inside the top of the door which said Pool Parlour.

I dropped the paper into a lamp-post trash can, pushed open the door and went up the green-carpeted staircase. The air was close and stale in here; smelling of days-old cigarette smoke and canned beer. I followed the well-trodden, stained carpet up two flights, past flaking brown-painted doors until I came out on a landing ending in a frosted glass screen. It had Pool Parlour across it in black, semi-Gothic lettering.

I pushed open the swing-door. A man with a greasy face, wearing a green and black striped shirt sat at a table with a bottle of whisky at his elbow. My man was at the far end of the parlour; there were about five tables, full-size with green-shaded lamps hanging over them. It was fairly dark in here, but the lights were on at the table farthest from me. A few men sat along benches at the side of the room and talked or read papers; as an entertainment it wasn't much. The man at the door talked out the corner of his mouth.

'You want a game, mister?'

'Just visiting,' I said.

He sighed. 'That's what I figured.'

I went on down the room to the far table. My man was lining up his cue ball with the spot, making an elaborate fist of it. As I got near to him I saw that Mrs Benson hadn't exaggerated. If it was Cheney, that is. He was a good-looking young man, but his face was weak. His heavy black hair was immaculately parted; he wore soft leather chukka boots under his narrow trousers. His hands, I saw as he cued the first shot, were well-kept but soft; he wore a thin, red silk tie, neatly knotted in under the collar of his black and white stripe shirt. That was silk too. I came up behind him and waited until he had finished the shot. He chipped the spot but his own ball failed to make the corner pocket. With that technique he would have missed the L.A. freeway tunnel.

'Mr Cheney?'

He nodded, like he knew me. 'Like a game?' he said.

'Just ten minutes of your time,' I said.

I flashed him my licence in the plastic holder. It may have been my imagination but I thought his face changed colour. On the other hand it may have been the light in here. I put the photostat wallet back in my pocket. We went and sat down on one of the benches at the side of the long room. It was quiet up this end; the big steam pipes which ran along behind the benches gave an occasional creak, loud in the silence.

'I believe you're a friend of Carmen Benson,' I said.

He selected a cigarette out of a metal case he took from his inside pocket. He didn't offer me one. He finished lighting the cigarette before he answered.

'I knew her,' he said cautiously. He didn't meet my eyes.

'I heard it a little differently to that,' I said.

'You must have been talking to Sheriff

Clark,' he said with some heat. 'I told him all I know. I don't have to answer your questions.'

'You don't,' I said, 'but you might find it more convenient.'

'Meaning what?' he said.

'Meaning that I can take short cuts where the police can't. For instance, like finding a witness who saw you and the Benson girl together that Saturday afternoon.'

This was a pure fabrication on my part, thrown up just for the hell of it, but it had a fantastic effect on Cheney. The cigarette fell from his suddenly trembling lips and hit a chain of fiery sparks on the dirty linoleum floor. He turned towards me with a face that looked as muddy as the Agano that morning. I bent down and picked up the cigarette and placed it on one edge of the pool table, where it wouldn't burn the wood.

'How the hell could you?' he blurted out. 'There was no-one . . . ' He stopped the stumbling flow of words and his face turned pink. There was a heavy silence. The old guy way up at the door looked towards us, his features a white blur in the gloom.

'So you did see her that afternoon,' I said.

'Aw, go to hell, Faraday,' he said thickly. 'You don't know anything.'

'I can't prove it at the moment,' I said. I got to my feet and looked down at his angry, twitching face. 'Talk to me or the Sheriff.'

He got up too and faced me. His knuckles showed white on the pool cue. I side-stepped quickly and picked up one of the balls from the table. He lifted the cue above his head and then all the life seemed to go out of him. The breath came from his mouth in a loud puff of disgust and he threw the cue down on the leather bench at his side. He sat down and put his head in his hands. I walked off towards the door. I hadn't gone two yards when I heard steps and felt his hand on my arm.

'Wait, Mr Faraday.' His face was agitated. Close up, he looked near to tears.

'It isn't that I don't want to co-operate.

The truth is that I can't tell you what you want to know.'

'The choice is yours,' I said.

'Will you hold off for twenty-four hours?' he said. He couldn't meet my gaze.

'Cream puffs like you nauseate me,' I told him. 'Have you any idea what the Bensons are going through?'

He bit his lip and the pink was back in his face.

'I can't tell you anything and that's straight,' he said. 'And don't come around the garage any more. I've got my living to earn.'

'Suit yourself,' I said. 'I'll be back. I think you'll be glad to tell the truth by the time Tom Clark's finished. They tell me Carmen Benson was a real nice girl.'

I got to the door when I heard his cue smash on the edge of the pool table. The loafers on the benches went in a sudden rush towards Cheney's end of the room. The man on the door got up and started swearing. I went out and down the stairs. The air felt much cleaner in the street.

*   *   *

It was around half-past eight. The wind was rising in gusts and icy spats of rain tapped at the windows. I lay on my bed at the Pinetop Motel, rattled the ice in the bottom of my whisky glass and stared at the ceiling. The central heating gave out a pleasant warmth and the shaded lamps reinforced the feeling I should be getting soft with too much of this. So I wasn't really sorry when the phone buzzed around a quarter to nine.

It was Grunwohl. 'Call from L.A., Mr Faraday. You want it put through?'

'Sure,' I said. Why wouldn't I want it put through?

'How you making out, Mike?' It was Stella.

'So-so,' I said. 'Looks like it's going to be a tough one.'

I asked her to ring up Dame Dora in the morning and report limited progress. She had a right to something for her money. I reached for a cigarette while we talked. I trailed the phone on its extension cord and went over to the window and pulled the heavy drapes.

'You might check on a girl called Patti Morgan,' I told Stella. 'Works with the missing girl but omitted to tell me she also lives in Mudville. She came home with the Benson kid the night before she got lost. Might be nothing in it. Again, you never know.'

Stella took a note while I smoked on and examined one of the sporting prints on the wall. It showed an old guy being brought home on a hurdle, by folks in top hats and riding breeches. It was called 'Return From the Hunt.' I knew how he felt. I've been that way myself. But not after hunting.

'What about Holgren?' I asked Stella.

'I was coming to that,' she said patiently. 'He was a lawyer here in L.A. Very highly respected and all that. Possible link is one of his principal clients, a General Diaz who lives on a big place just outside Mudville. I haven't had time to check on Diaz.'

'Good girl,' I said. Holgren wasn't my case but the extra information wouldn't hurt. Diaz might bear looking into.

'Look after yourself, Mike,' she said.

'Sure,' I said. 'Like always.'

I put down the phone and finished my cigarette. I got up and leafed through the Mudville phone book. I was afraid it might be ex-directory but I found Diaz lived at a house named The Palisades at a place called Barrett's Heights. I decided to pay him a visit. That would be ex-directory too. At the back of the phone book there was a large-scale map of Mudville and the surrounding area. Barrett's Heights looked to be about four miles on the other side of town.

I checked on the Smith-Wesson. The barrel was only a two-inch, but when I screwed the silencer on it made the whole set-up pretty long. Even so my special holster with the spring clip fitting made for a fast draw. It was always my one fear that the bulk of the silencer would impede the draw but so far it hadn't happened. And a silencer was highly desirable in my line of business.

The shoulder-holster made a nice feel against my under-arm as I got in the Buick and drove out. It was raining sheets again but it might dry off with the wind. I stopped on the ramp, pulled the chain and let the garage door down. The parking lot was full as I gunned out of the Motel. Ever since I checked in I had promised myself a pleasant evening in the bar lowering highballs and listening to the rain battering the windows but something always conspired to stop me.

I drove quickly into town. There was nothing about on the roads; the rain wasn't any encouragement to pleasure motoring. I noticed most of the houses I passed had their TV sets on. It was probably Groucho Marx night. By the time I got into the middle of town the rain had stopped. On the other side of town I looked at the map again. The turning was a clearly-marked one and it was a good road, well tarmaced and wide.

Presently I came to another fork with a big black and white sign; it pointed right again and directed me to Barrett's Heights. Not surprisingly, the Buick had her nose uphill by this time and great clumps of trees, including cypress and pine, were waving in the high wind as my headlamps passed across them. I got down in low gear, switched off the main beam and crawled along the last half-mile. No sense in advertising my presence, though the wind would have covered the sound of the motor.

After a while I came to a high brick wall surrounding some big estate. Then I passed fancy iron gates set between brick pillars. There was a lodge on one side of the gates with light coming out of the windows. I drove on for several hundred yards. I pulled the car on to a grass verge under the shadow of the wall, switched off the side-lights and killed the motor. I went pussy-footing back through the wet grass to the lodge entrance. There were houses opposite but they weren't lighted.

The gates were padlocked. Over the entrance, suspended from the brick pillars, was a sign in wrought iron which spelled out The Palisades. I looked over at the lodge. The front rooms were on a level with the gates. Bright lights burned and there were no drapes across the windows. Even as I watched the figure of a man passed across the panes. It was too risky that way. I went back to the car; I picked out my pencil flash from the dash cubby-hold and went around the back and unlocked the boot. I had a coil of rope in there for emergency. I hooked it over my arm and took it along just in case.

Then I set out to walking in the opposite direction, in the darkness made by the height of the wall. My trousers and the skirts of my raincoat were soon soaked by the grass. The wall seemed to go on for ever and just as I was thinking of going back to the car it disappeared behind some bushes; I risked a glimpse with the flash and saw there was a path between the bushes and the wall. I followed this along for another hundred yards; the wall went at a right-angle and was then replaced by a simple fence made of nailed two by four timbers. I climbed the fence without any difficulty and found myself in a tangle of trees and low bushes.

Another brick wall came up in front; this was broken in one place and a half-hearted attempt had been made to patch the gap with baulks of sawn pine. I left the rope coil and shinned over. I was in thick orchard ground, the trees spaced at four yard intervals; the thick, untended grass and the low-hanging branches of the soaking trees made the going even more heavy than before.

When I left the orchard the thin, diffused light from the moon, straggling behind the dark clouds, glinted briefly on glass. I crept through a row of hothouses, skirted a low box hedge and found myself out on lawn. A long way off the lights of the lodge showed through the trees. I padded on across the lawn to a tarmac area; it formed part of the drive which curved up from the lodge gates towards the house. Either there were no lights in the house itself or the trees were too thick but I couldn't see a thing of The Palisades.

I walked quietly back from the drive and went in under the trees again. I had just got into the shadow when the lights of a car came up the road outside from the direction of Mudville. It stopped at the lodge gates but the motor kept on running. I heard a car door slam and then voices; someone came out of the lodge. An orange oblong of light leaked from the kitchen of the house and then a man's figure crossed it. I went back farther under the trees. I knelt down behind an ornamental bush and watched. The faint chink of iron came up to me as the gates were opened; there were more muffled voices and the car door slammed again.

The headlights slashed across the bush and I ducked back. The car drove round a curve in the drive and disappeared. I followed the lights through the trees for a moment or two more and then they died. I stayed put for about a quarter of an hour but nothing else moved. The light in the room of the lodge nearest to me went out. I was getting cramped and the wet grass was soaking my trousers so I eased up.

I crossed the lawn at a run, keeping from tree to tree. I slipped as I got behind a large oak and pulled up sharp as I caught its rough bark. I hadn't heard the soft pad on the turf behind me; as it was, my abrupt halt served a useful purpose. A black streak of thunder went by me in the

94

gloom, muscles full stretch, a low-powered rumble deep in its throat. The big Dobermann rounded a full ten yards away with effortless thrusts of its spread paws and headed back towards me, the faint light from the sky reflecting on its eyeballs.

I had the Smith-Wesson out by this time and had already set off in a zig-zagging run in the general direction of the wall. I could hear the large pads of the guard dog gaining effortlessly on me; it still didn't give tongue and I threw myself sideways round the dark bole of a tree. I heard its paws scratch heavily on the bark a second later.

As the dog rebounded from the tree, I found my bearings and set to doubling about to throw him off; this could obviously be only a limited strategy and my breath was going fast. I came up over a rise, with only a head start over the animal and was then going full tilt down-hill with very little idea of what was in front of me. The dog sprang at the same moment that I saw the branch about eight feet off the ground; I jumped for it, caught it one-handed and swung in a violent arc, all the strain on my right arm.

The Dobermann's body bounced against me as he went by, the jaws snapped and he sheared away an inch or two from the bottom hem of my raincoat. I heard him land with a snarling crash in the bushes; I pushed the revolver back into my holster with my left hand and I got two hands over the branch and levered myself up. Sharp teeth clashed in the air a good three feet below me as the Dobermann jumped again.

Then things started to happen quickly. The lodge lights went on, there was the barking of dogs in the far distance and some sort of siren started up. The Dobermann sounded puzzled; he faced around in the direction of the lodge gates but still didn't bark. Lights came on through the trees; the whole house was aroused. When a chain of lamps blazed on the drive, turning the whole place into daylight, I thought it was about time I got the hell out.

The Dobermann was still looking towards the drive when I hit him; from ten feet up my six feet three must have seemed like the sky falling on him. I only hoped I hadn't broken his back but I could already hear voices and see torches from the direction of my retreat; somebody was searching the area under the wall. The Dobermann went flat in the middle and his breath went out in a protesting yelp. I laid the butt of the Smith-Wesson across his head, behind the ear a couple of times with all the force I could muster. It's best to use the barrel but I didn't want to break the silencer off, or leave it behind me. Anyways, it didn't make much difference to the Dobermann. He went flat out for the night as I gave him a third one for luck.

I went off then across the lawn, took the low hedge near the kitchen garden like Jesse Owens and made for the gap in the wall. I had just got round one of the hot-houses when I ran full-tilt into a man carrying a torch directed low down on the ground. He must have switched it on the instant he heard my footsteps. He gave an exclamation like he had something urgent to tell me but he was pretty resourceful at that. He took a sideswipe at me with something that caught a glancing blow to the side of my head; flashes of brilliant light sparked off in front of my face and I went down. My head cleared almost instantly and I caught him round the knees.

I put all my weight into it and he crashed over with a loud cry of surprise. I was up again then. All I could see of him was brown trousers and tan shoes. I shook the muzziness out of my head and went off again as quick as a worker leaving the factory. A moment later I was very close to the wall where I had come into the grounds. There was quite a palaver going on near the main gate and I could see lights and figures dashing about in the reflected glow. I wondered why they didn't unleash the dogs.

My knees gave way when I came in under the trees and I realized that the knock on the head had been harder than I thought. When I came to again the dogs were barking, the lights still visible through the trees but no-one came near me. I was lying propped against a soft mass. The smell of wet grass was in my nostrils; that and a scent that was cloying, familiar and unmistakeable.

I clawed myself upwards; my fingers met unresisting grass, pieces of stick, leaves and such-like. I sat up. I had fallen against a large compost heap under the low trees near the main wall of the grounds; a place where gardeners dumped grass cuttings and other debris in summer but which had become something else this dark November night. As I got up my fingers had seized automatically on a substance which neither gave nor tore.

I pulled against an immovable weight. My exploring fingers felt a considerable bulk. I got out my pencil flash, cupped it with my hands and risked a quick beam. What I had hold of was a segment of a woman's green tweed skirt.

I put out the light and felt upwards, clearing and raking with my hands. After a moment more I found a surface cold and soft. I risked the light again and almost dropped the torch. Though the eyes and nostrils were filled with mould and corruption, insects and worms had been at work beneath, there was still enough left of the face for me to recognize the unflawed likeness that rested in my wallet. Carmen Benson had come home.

# 6

## Mannlicher

I went over the wall like a school kid coming out of a classroom. Behind me the racket died. I scooped up the coil of rope as I passed. When I got out of the Diaz place I edged round behind the bushes and stopped. Lights were still shining up near the lodge but I couldn't hear any more noise. Even the dogs weren't barking. I put the rope in the car boot.

The Buick was facing away from The Palisades. I got my shoulder to the windscreen upright and pushed her off the grass verge. She rolled easily. I ran with her for a few yards and then edged behind the wheel as she gathered speed down the gentle slope. We got away nice and quietly. When The Palisades had dropped way behind I switched on the ignition and put her softly into third to start the engine; she turned over and I let her drift down the road. Only then did I switch on the sidelights.

I looked at my watch. Incredibly, it was only just coming up to a quarter to eleven. Two corpses in two days, both found by the same patsy was too true to be good, as Bernard Shaw put it. Sheriff Clark already had reservations about me; he was going to have a field day with this one.

Presently I came to a fork in the road. After ten minutes I saw lights and found I was on the other side of town. I soon picked up the road I wanted and that saw me back to the Pinetop. This time I left the car outside and let myself in through the front door of No. Seventeen with my key. It had started raining again.

In the bathroom I looked at myself in the mirror. My face was covered with dirt and mould; my trench coat had green patches from the grass and my shoes were caked with mud. I mixed myself a Scotch and water, using the bottle I'd ordered from room service the night before. There was an ice-box in the suite and when I'd put a couple of cubes in the glass and got the first taste, raw and smoky in my mouth, I felt I might live.

I sponged off the raincoat and attended to the shoes while I ran the bath. I found the Smith-Wesson had blood and animal hairs on the butt. I must have hit the Dobermann harder than I figured. By the time I had repaired the damage I was starting to think reasonably again; I decided to give Sheriff Clark a ring when I got out of the tub. He would have to know sooner or later and it would look better coming from me. And I had to have some law in if I intended to do something about General Diaz.

When I got through it was midnight. I dressed, went back into the bedroom, put the holster under my arm and mixed myself another drink. The trench coat was dry now; the small tear under the edge of the hem didn't show so I put it on, got back into the car and drove into Mudville through the rain. If ever a town tried it was doing its best to live up to its name.

Macklehenny finished pounding and slid the third statement sheet out of his typewriter.

'That's about it,' he grunted.

I read the statement through slowly. I didn't have to alter anything.

'Sign here,' he said. He pushed a pen towards me.

'You'd better get some more sheets ready,' I said. 'We haven't finished yet.'

'Oh,' he said.

Just then the door opened and Sheriff Clark came in. He looked angry about something. He went over towards the stove and held out his hands above the doors. He hung up his revolver belt over the hat-stand and stamped back towards me. Then I saw that he was wearing thick leather thigh boots. It reminded me of his brown trousers and tan shoes. For some reason that worried me. I started to revise my story.

'You've changed your shoes,' I said without thinking.

He frowned. 'Sure,' he said. 'Any

104

objections? I always keep a change in the car. I been tramping around some in the wet tonight.'

He trashed over towards his desk and sat down morosely. He stuck the briar pipe in his face and fished around for a match. Macklehenny slung him a box. Clark didn't seem to be watching but a lean hand plucked the box out of the air. He got the pipe drawing to his satisfaction and sat back in his old chair belching out clouds of smoke. He looked like Eastman Kodak's chemical division on a Saturday night. He sifted through my statement and wrinkled up his face. He read it very carefully from end to end and then put it back on the desk.

'You didn't come here this time of night just for that,' he said.

'Too true,' I said. 'You're not going to like this, Sheriff.'

'Precious little in the news you bring to like,' he said sourly.

'I got another corpse for you,' I said. 'Unless it's been reported already.'

The silence that followed was like the explosion of a bomb. Clark cleared his

105

throat with an ominous rumble.

'This is where I came in,' said Macklehenny. He spread out his hands to Sheriff Clark in a despairing gesture.

'No-one reports anything important to me. I got two lost dog calls and a missing car so far tonight.'

Clark ignored him. His eyes were curiously bright. He took the pipe out of his mouth. 'Come again.'

'I found the Benson girl,' I said. 'She's dead. Buried in a rubbish tip. I didn't get to see any details.'

Clark breathed heavily. His face was drained of colour in the yellow lighting of the office. He made a short stabbing gesture with the stem of his pipe.

'Go on,' he said. 'When did all this happen?'

'Earlier tonight,' I said.

Macklehenny glanced up at the wall clock. 'How early?' he said.

'About two hours ago,' I said. I looked back at Clark. He rubbed his nose with the edge of his forefinger.

'You took your time about reporting it,' he said mildly.

'I drove around to think things out,' I said. 'It didn't look good two nights in a row.'

Clark smiled thinly. 'You got a point there. Question is, where?'

'I was afraid you'd ask that,' I said. 'This one is out at General Diaz' place. Looks like she's been dead ever since she disappeared.'

I thought Clark was going to blow up then but he kept his rising anger bottled in.

'General Diaz?' he said. 'Well, well, Faraday, you sure know how to pick 'em. I think you'd better start at the beginning.'

He turned to Macklehenny. 'Roust out Doc Ellsworth, before he turns in.'

He glanced back at me and added out of the corner of his mouth, 'Unless this one's disappeared too.'

I ignored the irony. 'My secretary rang in this evening,' I told Clark. 'She'd checked on Holgren and found he was a lawyer in L.A. acting for General Diaz.'

Clark put another match to his pipe, which had gone out.

'I could have told you that,' he said calmly.

'Well, you didn't,' I said, 'and as I have to make my living by getting my information the best way I can, I asked her to see what she could dig up. I'd come to a dead end for the moment in the Benson business, so I thought I'd have a run out there. I had a hunch the girl's disappearance and Holgren's murder might be connected — and I hit the jackpot.'

Clark smoked moodily on; in the background I could hear Macklehenny on the phone. He seemed to be having trouble convincing the doc it was urgent.

'The General's place didn't look too hospitable,' I said.

'So you got in over the wall,' he finished for me.

I must have looked surprised for he went on, 'The General has a good reason for not wanting visitors. So then?'

'I hung about decorating the bushes,' I said, 'and an oversized Airedale took a bite at my rear end and I had to lay him out. That stirred the place up. Someone

108

else was up there too. I don't think he had anything to do with the house. He hit me over the head.'

I looked at the Sheriff; it may have been my imagination but I thought he seemed uncomfortable. Macklehenny put the phone down. I glanced at Clark's boots again. He only puffed on his pipe and faced me squarely.

'So?'

'I crawled away,' I said. 'I must have been half-dazed. When I came to I was lying on a compost heap. I uncovered a woman's skirt. It was the Benson girl — buried.'

'You know how she got killed?' said Macklehenny.

'She didn't tell me,' I said. 'I didn't have time for a post mortem. I went over the wall pretty quick.'

Macklehenny cleared his throat derisively.

'Seems to me General Diaz has a lot of explaining to do,' I said.

'Never mind about that,' said Clark with surprising sharpness. 'For a stranger around here you turn up with some

109

incredible information.'

'Here we go,' I said. 'While we sit chewing the fat the evidence may have disappeared again.'

'Private property,' he said. 'Can't go on private property without a warrant.'

'Jeezechrise,' I said. 'Who is this General Diaz? Does he own the whole town?'

'Just about,' said Macklehenny. He didn't sound like he was joking either.

A spark of humour came into Clark's frosty eyes. He grinned at my expression.

'Simmer down,' he said. 'We're waiting for the doc. Then we'll take a look out there.'

'In the meantime I should get the town signboard changed,' I said.

Macklehenny chuckled softly behind me, 'You're all right, Faraday,' he said.

Clark got up and strapped on his Colt again. Macklehenny put on a black and white checked lumber jacket and sat down at his desk. Clark came back and resumed his seat. He looked at me searchingly.

'Feel this,' I said. I got hold of his

fingers and put his hand on the side of my head. There was a big lump coming up there. He jumped like he'd been electrocuted.

'O.K.', he said, taking his hand away in a hurry. 'I didn't say I disbelieved you. We're going out there, aren't we?'

'So you say,' I said. 'Or are we waiting to give time for General Diaz to clear up his garden?'

'You're stepping over the line there, Mr Faraday,' said Macklehenny. He sounded aggrieved.

'Sorry, Sheriff,' I told Clark. 'I've had a rough couple of evenings since I hit town.'

'No offence,' said Clark. 'You just don't know the setup, that's all.'

'You calling in the County boys?'

He shook his head. 'This is my town and my jurisdiction,' he said. 'Ain't nothing we can't handle right here. I had two killings on my patch before.'

'You know your own business best,' I said.

'Too right he does,' said Macklehenny. He got up and went over to the hat-stand

**111**

and buckled on his own revolver belt. The sound of a car-horn came from outside.

'That'll be the doc,' said Clark. 'Let's go. You ask him to pick up the others?'

The last question was to the deputy; Macklehenny nodded. We went out down the corridor. Clark locked the door behind us. The square was empty except for a large black sedan and an inconspicuous-looking truck with a canvas hood. I found out later it contained a generator, another two deputies and a police photographer. Clark could do things quietly when he had a mind to. The Sheriff went over to the sedan. The doctor was an elderly man with a thatch of grey hair and a twisted, melancholy face. He jerked his head briefly in our direction. Clark came back and joined us.

'We'll take your car,' he said. 'And remember this, Faraday. If it is the Benson girl, we're sitting on this for a day or two. That's why I only got a handful of people along. There'll be enough about Holgren in the paper tomorrow morning. O.K.?'

'O.K.', I said. 'Publicity won't help me much, either.'

He smiled. I got in the driving seat of the Buick, Clark got in beside me and Macklehenny in the rear. The doctor started his engine and drove off, I pulled in behind him and the truck followed us. We sneaked out of town nice and quiet.

* * *

The generator throbbed and vibrated in the darkness, an occasional spat of rain sizzled on the arc lamps and we stood in a semi-circle and watched the doctor at work where the arcs cut a white hole in the dark. What was left of Carmen Benson lay on a tarpaulin and little white-haired Doc Ellsworth grunted and wheezed to himself as he rooted among the sodden clothing. He took a sharp knife from one of the deputies and started cutting cloth away. There was a heavy, pungent odour on the night air.

'Jeeze,' said one of the deputies; he was standing down-wind. He shifted away and came up towards us. He looked white.

Clark stood near me with his wind-cheater zipped up and a grim expression on his face. We stood near the wall of the Diaz place, not far from where I'd found the girl. Cables snaked over the wall to the truck outside. Apart from the Doc, there was just Clark, Macklehenny, a deputy called Flinton, the photographer and myself. The other deputy was at the lodge.

It was two a.m. I lit another cigarette and stood back in the shadow of the wall. I couldn't understand why Clark didn't knock up the Diaz household and start taking the place apart. I was finding this a bit different from L.A. But maybe Clark had his own reasons for what he did. I looked at him sharply. He stood quite at ease, one arm hooked over the low branch of an apple-tree, and smoked his pipe. The glow from the bowl gave his face a sardonic quality it didn't have in daylight.

Clark stirred; he knocked the pipe against the trunk of the tree, sending a tiny chain of fire dancing to the ground.

'Don't look so worried, Faraday,' he said. 'It'll all come clear as we go along.'

'There's a few things bothering me about this set-up,' I said. 'That's aside from the minor point of who's taken a dislike to the local inhabitants.'

Clark put another match to his pipe; flames danced, throwing his face into high relief.

'Meaning what?' he said.

'The General Diaz end of the deal,' I said. 'Holgren's his lawyer; he gets his brains beaten out. This Benson girl gets killed in his garden. There's various trivial things like me getting hit over the head. Yet you can't seem to work up enough curiosity to go up to the house and ask if they've seen any bodies lying around.'

'Let's get one thing straight, Mr Faraday,' said Clark, moving easily out from under the tree. 'Maybe you didn't hear so good what I said back in the office. This is my town, and I'm in charge here. You got no official standing at all. If you want to make a fool of yourself, go on up to the house. But they won't let you in and you certainly won't get to see General Diaz without my sayso. You'll just have to trust me or we ain't got no deal.

This is a small town and we'll play it my way or not at all. It's up to you.'

'Guess you know your own business best,' I said. 'But it seems a queer way of going about it.'

'Our ways may not be L.A. ways, son,' he said kindly, 'but you'll see results if you stick around long enough.'

We were interrupted by a dry cough from Ellsworth; he'd gotten up from the tarpaulin and was standing impatiently behind us. He held something in a blood-stained handkerchief. 'She was killed by a high-velocity rifle bullet,' he said. 'It hit her in the side and travelled upwards, bursting the heart before stopping. From my experience of wounds I'd say it was something like a Mannli-cher. We'll know more in the morning. I've done all I propose to do here tonight. You can have her moved to Johnstown whenever you're ready.'

'Thanks, doc,' said Clark. 'Phone me a preliminary report just as soon as you can. And keep this under tabs.'

The doctor snorted. 'What do you take me for?' he said, going back towards the

116

floodlights. 'Anyone would think this was my first experience of violent death.'

Clark grinned. 'Take no notice,' he said to me. 'He always carries on like this.'

He walked over and stood looking down at the body. 'That's it, boys,' he said finally, 'you can start packing up. The ambulance should be here any time.'

The main lights went out suddenly and Clark and Macklehenny and I started picking our way back towards the lodge; the deputy led the way with the torch. The photographer stayed behind with the body; he kept one flood switched on. The Doc was still mumbling to himself.

'I'll make a deal with you,' I told Clark. 'I've got an idea I'd like to work on — and I want to see the Cheney lad again. In the meantime you get General Diaz' story. Then we'll compare notes.'

'Can't do no harm,' said Clark. 'But we shan't have long. This second one will blow the town wide open. And the Press will bring in floods of sightseers.'

We got up near the lodge gates as we finished. The cars were parked there. Light came out of all the windows of the lodge. Clark drew me to one side. Macklehenny went ahead with the doctor. I could hear the rattle of metal as someone unlocked the gates.

'Listen, Mr Faraday,' said Clark. 'I'd like you to do me a favour if you would.'

'I've guessed already, Sheriff,' I said. 'I thought I'd go and see the Bensons anyway. It might be better coming from a stranger. I'll call in tomorrow night after my other chores.'

Clark nodded. He put his hand on my arm. 'Thanks, Mr Faraday. I really appreciate this. I'm not much good at that sort of thing.'

'Glad to help,' I said though I wasn't looking forward to it. We got back in my car. The ambulance passed us before we had gone a mile. It seemed like a long way back to town.

# 7

## The Bowman

I sat in the restaurant-bar of the Pinetop and did justice to black coffee and buckwheat cakes with syrup. The bar-tender looked cheerful. He came over to the table.

'Say, you sure brought some life to this place,' he said enthusiastically. 'I told you the centre of town was where all the action was.'

He tapped a copy of an L.A. paper; it showed a picture of me and Clark standing against the sedan below a foot of black type screaming about the Holgren murder.

'Sure,' I said, 'you weren't kidding. They got plenty of death too. You want to look out for tomorrow's sheet if you think that's something.'

His smile faded.

'I did the job myself,' I said. 'Sheriff

119

Clark doesn't know about it yet. Keep it under your hat.'

'Sure, Mr Faraday.' The bar-keep gulped a little. He didn't know whether to laugh or break into a gallop. Just then Grunwohl came into the bar. He nodded frostily at the bar-keep.

'Don't let me detain you,' he snapped. The bar-tender walked over to the bar and started polishing glasses.

Grunwohl leaned over my table. 'Just thought I'd remind you, Mr Faraday, that your credit runs out today. If you want to stay on you'll have to re-register.'

'I'll come along to the office after breakfast,' I said. 'You'd better book me in for another week. This looks like being a long one.'

Grunwohl glanced at the paper which the bar-keep had left on the table.

'Dreadful thing for the town,' he said disapprovingly. He sounded like I should have left Holgren in the gutter and not have bothered to report it.

'Murder's always bad for trade,' I said sympathetically. Grunwohl stared at me and then went out. The bar-keep sauntered back for his paper. He stared after Grunwohl. A suppressed sneer was fighting to get out. Finally he didn't struggle against it any more.

'There's character in that face,' he said eventually. 'I don't know where it's got to, but it must be there somewhere.'

I grinned and went on with my breakfast. When I finished I went down to Grunwohl's office and got rid of some more greenbacks; he made Scrooge seem like a spendthrift the way he put the bills in his safe. I figured he was the sort of man who wires his notes into his wallet. Then I got the Buick and drove out of town; the wind felt like it had razor blades in it.

I parked the car way past the lodge gates; there was no sign of life there but I wasn't interested in General Diaz this morning. I went along the road until I came to the houses opposite; there were two or three big villas set back from the road with broad, well-kept lawns, shaded by large trees which must have been an impressive sight in summer. The fourth house was the one I wanted.

It was almost opposite the lodge gates, but hidden entirely by trees and thick undergrowth; all one could see from the road was the white-painted top of a very tall building. Then I got lucky. In between the two entrance posts, set back from the gravelled drive on a narrow strip of lawn was a large white-painted board. In black Old English lettering it said; Fitzgeorge Country Club. Dancing. Residential Accommodation.

I set out walking up the drive. The place was laid out like a formal English garden with beech trees spreading wide branches over the muddy-looking winter lawns. At the end of the drive it split into two walks; to the left the gravelled path continued along the side of a lake. The right led to the house; two low wings joined to the central section which was built in Colonial style, with a vast pillared porch in front.

I picked out a window I thought would do, on the next to topmost storey; not too high, but high enough to clear the trees. I went up the central steps and rang the bell on the porch. The door was opened by a square-faced woman with a sharp look. I could have sworn she had twenty-twenty vision, though she wore glasses as big as manhole covers.

'My wife and I are looking for a place to stay for a few days,' I said.

She looked at me suspiciously. 'A bit late for a holiday, isn't it?'

'Have you got a room or haven't you?' I said.

She seemed taken aback. She sniffed to cover her confusion. 'Come in,' she said, holding the door wide. It was a large hall inside, with white-panelled walls, furnished with good quality reproduction Colonial pieces.

'We'd like something fairly high up, facing front,' I said. She gave me another deadpan look. 'We got some good rooms on the first floor,' she said. 'It's a fair ways up to the top and there's no lift.'

'That's all right,' I said. 'There's no need for you to come.'

Her expression seemed to soften then. 'Well,' she said, more to herself than to me, 'the bell-boy's helping to drain out the swim-pool or I'd ask him to show you.

It's out of season, you see.'

She waited indecisively, the fingers of one lean hand drumming on a carved table.

'Well, I guess it won't matter much, if you don't mind seeing yourself up,' she said. She took a couple of keys off a board covered with metal hooks; there must have been more than seventy rooms for guests.

'Number fifty-nine fourth floor front centre, number seventy fifth floor,' she said. Her eyes almost sparkled. 'Hope you find what you're looking for.'

'Thanks,' I said politely. 'I'll only be a minute.'

I went up the broad, old-fashioned staircase. She stood in the hall looking up at me until I turned the corner of the stairhead. The decent decor extended to the upper floors. There was a good carpet in all the corridors. The lay-out had that out of season atmosphere; even the smell was out of season. The landings were too warm and dry with that never-opened-window feeling; the closets I passed were probably full of linen put away for the winter. There was no sound from behind the closed doors. Everything was dead and long done for.

I found number fifty-nine without any trouble. As soon as I got inside the door I knew I wouldn't have to go up to the room above. This room would have done real fine. It was an elegant apartment with carved furniture and a massive reproduction four-poster with a canopy over it. Half of the window was taken up by a bulky rosewood dressing table with brass handles. I stood frowning at it.

Then I went down on the carpet. I worked my way along the skirting first. It all depended really on whether the dressing table had been moved and if it had, whether any impressions remained. I tested the weight with my hand; it was heavy enough. Presently I found very faint indentations left by the feet in the carpet; the thing had been moved to one side of the window. Then I went back towards the centre again. There were deep impressions in the carpet to the right of each leg. Someone had moved the table temporarily and then put it back slightly out of alignment.

Though the window panes were a blurred mess with the rain, the casement moved upwards in smooth runners. I could see the whole of General Diaz' estate from here. Everything lined up if you worked from a certain angle. The lower floors of the big Gothic mansion with its mock-Georgian porch could be glimpsed only through the scrubby winter trees but the upper storeys were clear and stood out in sharp detail.

I could even see a figure at one of the windows. It moved away into the gloom beyond as I caught sight of it. But a good pair of field glasses would have done the trick. I felt quite pleased with myself. I looked on the edges of the sill; it was too much to expect that I should find scratches. There were some there, but old, judging by their appearance. I got down near the sill; I could smell a faint pungency that even the dampness of the rain-soaked garden couldn't entirely dispel. When I rubbed my hand across the woodwork, a slight blackness remained on my fingers. I put down the window and relocked it with pardonable smugness. I went out and almost waltzed down the staircase.

Miss Dill-Pickle of 1929 looked almost human when I handed her the keys.

'You didn't find any trace of your wife, did you?' she said gently. 'I could have told you we've had no young lady staying here during the past few weeks.'

I must have looked confused, because I hadn't a hell of an idea what she was talking about.

'How did you guess?' I said mechanically, before the answer came to me.

'I've been in this business a long time, young man,' she said, searching my face with dark eyes. 'I get to know these things.'

'I see,' I said. 'Thanks, anyway.'

'You won't be wanting the room, will you?' she said.

'Not now,' I said truthfully.

'I quite understand,' she said, putting a sympathetic hand on my arm. She opened the door for me.

'I hope you find her,' she said, as I went down the porch steps. I guess my hunched shoulders must have looked like I was trying to fight back the tears of a deserted husband. Except that I was struggling to prevent myself from busting out laughing. I didn't want to spoil the old lady's faith in her sagacity.

When I had straightened my face I was almost up to the car. A girl was standing by it looking at the rear number plate. She wore black walking slacks and had a not altogether unattractive figure from what I could see of it under her pale blue windcheater.

The bright yellow bell of her hair told me who it was before she turned round.

'Hi, there,' said Patti Morgan brightly.

★  ★  ★

Close-up, I saw that she was even more attractive than she had seemed in Dame Dora's office; of course I had been more intent on preserving my dignity than in taking an inventory, but now I had more time. Her eyes had a sparkle and her face a freshness that wasn't only due to the cold air.

128

'I live here. Remember?' she said.

'You didn't say so,' I told her.

She turned a wide-eyed face towards me. 'Didn't I really? But then you were too busy teaching Dame Dora the rudiments of judo, as I recall it.'

'How is the old lady?' I said hastily, passing on to safer ground.

'Fine,' she said, smoothing down an imaginary out of place hair on her immaculate head. 'She gave me a couple of days off to see my folks.'

'Her way of keeping tabs on me?' I said.

She shook her head vigorously. 'Not at all, Mr Faraday. Dame Dora doesn't work like that. She gives absolute trust.'

'Sorry,' I said. 'My suspicious mind.'

She laughed. 'You don't look like a detective.'

'What did you expect?' I said.

'Oh, I don't know,' she said. 'Outside of films and plays I've always pictured them as grubby little men listening at keyholes and spying on bedrooms in divorce cases. Private ones, that is.'

'I get some cases like that,' I said. 'You

want a lift somewhere?'

She looked away from me up towards The Palisades and the distant fringe of the dark trees.

'Well, I was out for the exercise, but I think I've done enough walking for one day.'

I opened the door for her and she got into the passenger seat. I caught a soft rustle as she sat down; I figured she was wearing stockings underneath her slacks. I don't know why but somehow that seemed quite an exciting idea. It must have been the cold weather. There was a glint in her eye as I shut the door, like she knew what I was thinking. I put in the gear and we rolled back towards town.

'How are you making out?' she asked.

'Nothing spectacular,' I lied. 'It's a tight little town.'

She smiled. 'You can say that again. Dad's been in business here over twenty-five years and we're considered foreigners.'

She leaned forward and got a cigarette out of a pack she took from the pocket of her anorak; I lit it for her from the dash lighter. She wrinkled her nose at me through the smoke.

'A terrible business about Mr Holgren. What with Carmen missing, the town's a sad place.'

'Did you know Holgren?' I asked.

She shook her head. 'Only by name. He was quite a big man in L.A., I believe. Dame Dora served on the committee of the Chamber of Commerce with him once. An awful way to die.'

She huddled into the depths of the anorak, though whether from the coldness of the air outside the Buick or from thinking about Mudville's mortality rate, I couldn't make out.

'You can drop me on the edge of town,' she said. 'I've got a few shopping calls to make.'

'You wouldn't care for a drink?' I said.

Her eyes were bright as she turned towards me in the shadow of the car interior. 'Try me,' she said.

I pulled up in front of one of the hotels in the town centre. It was the Adair-House. We got out and walked through into the lounge. There was a long horse-shoe bar at one end. A few people were sitting about looking like they had all day to spare. We sat down in a booth.

Patti Morgan eased herself out of the anorak. She wore a white sweater underneath. Her figure did quite a lot for it.

'How's Stella?' she said.

'I didn't know you'd met,' I said.

She smiled. 'Now and again. Shopping around in L.A.'

A white-coated waiter with a built-in plastic smile came up for our order. His delight went on and off like a neon sign. I ordered a lager for myself. Patti Morgan chose a sherry.

'You busy tonight?' she asked.

I thought of my room in the Pinetop, Grunwohl's brand of cheerfulness, Clark's antiseptic office and the rain coming down over it all. I didn't propose to spend all my evenings in Mudville crawling around in wet mould. Though I didn't show too much eagerness.

'Depends,' I said cautiously.

The waiter came back with the drinks. His smile opened up another three millimetres when I told him to keep the change. The beer tasted good.

'I cook the best steak in town,' Patti said. That clinched it.

'What time do we dine?' I asked.

'I'll give you the address,' she said. 'Around nine o'clock?'

'Thanks,' I said. 'You're quite a girl for handing out addresses.'

She laughed this time. 'No sense in hanging back. Small towns teach you that.'

I took an envelope out of my pocket and pushed her a pen. She wrote the address and gave it me back.

'I'm partial to a nice steak,' I said.

★  ★  ★

I left Patti Morgan outside the hotel. I drove back to the place I went the day before and got outside some coffee, a plate of grilled fish with French fries and blueberry pie with cream. The same waitress in the Dutch outfit greeted me like an old friend. It was only after my second cup of coffee that I looked at the envelope; the address was a place called Greenside Manor. I wondered what her parents would be like. I decided to be a hick, wear a presentable suit and take along something for her mother. I bought a big box of candy after I left the lunch counter.

Then I drove out to Barrett's Heights. I'd already been in the back way. It couldn't do any harm to try the entrance. I stopped in front of The Palisades lodge and blipped the horn; there was no response but the scuttering of birds' wings in a nearby bush. I was about to give another blast when a surly-looking man in a mackinaw jacket came out of the lodge. He was big-built. I particularly noticed he had a revolver in a shiny brown leather holster at his waist. It looked like a Colt. I cut the motor and got out of the car. We faced one another through the iron bars. Close up he looked just as tough but not quite so unpleasant.

'You got some business?' he said, screwing up his eyes as he looked me over. I noticed he kept his right hand near the butt of his gun.

'I'd like to see the General,' I said.

I passed him the photostat of my licence in the plastic holster, through the bars. He studied it a moment and then pushed it back to me.

'The General don't see visitors,' he said decisively.

'Ask him,' I said.

He shrugged again. 'Wait here.' He went back into the lodge. It seemed like a long wait. It must have been all of ten minutes. The cold was biting and the sky threatened rain. In the end I went back to the car and sat down. I almost started to reverse preparatory to going back to town. I was glad I didn't. I was almost as surprised as the gateman. He came out at a run and started unlocking the gate.

'He'll see you,' he said in an incredulous mumble. 'You carry a gun?' he asked.

'Not today,' I said.

'Anyways, I'd like you to come in the lodge,' he said. 'I got my orders.'

He opened the lodge door and I followed him in. The interior of the first room was just bare pine walls. The only furniture was a table and chair. Most of

135

the available space was covered by gun racks. The place was more like an armoury.

'Expecting trouble?' I asked.

He grinned. 'Nothing we can't handle.'

He stood me over against the window and ran an expert hand over me. He didn't forget the forearms or the calves of the legs. It was as good as I'd seen for many a long year.

'Clean,' he whispered, like he was astonished. 'Wait here.'

He went into an inner room but I could see him watching me in a mirror. He needn't have worried really; the rifles were all locked into the racks. I heard a tinkle as he picked up the phone. He came back rubbing his hands.

'Go right up,' he said. 'When you get to the main entrance ring the porch bell. They'll take it from there.'

'Thanks,' I said politely. I went back to my car. Standing near it was another big man in a black leather wind-cheater. He had a rifle under his arm and one of the big Dobermanns tugging at a leash in front of him. He whistled like he was out enjoying the afternoon air but it was obvious he was guarding the open gate. These boys didn't leave much to chance. The first man came out and stood by the gate waiting to lock it.

'You must have been cashier at the Bastille,' I told him.

He grinned again. I got into the Buick and gunned her up the drive. In the mirror I could see him lock the gates. The second guard looked after me, then he and the Dobermann went off across the lawn and under the trees. The drive was well kept and curved round in large arcs, bordered by thick bushes. It was dark here even though it was early afternoon. The drive was over a quarter of a mile long but it looped and curved back on itself. The lay-out would more than double the real distance from the main gate; this would give time to the people of the house. But time to do what?

There was another advantage too to this styling of the drive. A man on foot, with or without a rifle, could reach any point on it just as easily — or perhaps more easily — than a man in a car if he wanted to intercept it. And a dog would make twice the speed of a car over this terrain. At this point the Buick's nose was going up the last slope and I was in low gear again; the curves were so fierce that I had to go around at a walking pace. There wasn't room for another car to pass.

I noticed something else too; just before every bend were stationed old-style, long-shafted country carts. They were beautifully maintained; each stood on a trim shaved plot surrounded on three sides by low-chained enclosures. Each was a museum piece; their wheels were picked out in yellow and black and the brass fittings sparkled even in this damp atmosphere. More important still it would take only one man to roll them forward and block the drive. All faced slight downhill slopes, all were chocked with blocks of wood under the wheels. These were even fitted with rope toggles like they use on aircraft.

Question was did General Diaz want to keep people in? Or out? Either way the answer would be entertaining. I stopped the car near a set of massive steps flanked by Grecian-type statues, which led up into the shadowy porch. I rang the bell in a door which wouldn't have looked out of place at the Kremlin. A small peephole in the panel opened and a pair of cold eyes studied me; then bolts were drawn and I went on in.

The man who opened was tall and proportionately broad; he was dressed in fawn slacks and a khaki shirt open at the neck. The pips on the shoulders of the shirt made it look like a military uniform. Around his waist he had a canvas belt with a big-handled revolver butt protruding from a canvas holster. He had a strong, yellow-complexioned face and a heavy mustache. Dark glasses with side blinders covered his eyes. He impressed me as a durable, tough character.

'Mr Faraday.' He slurred the words in the Spanish style. His teeth were very white under his mustache. 'This way, please. Have the goodness to walk in front of me.'

He motioned me forward along the hall. We went up an oak staircase lined with oil paintings. It made The Prado

139

look like a two-bit provincial art gallery. The man in the side-blinders kept a hand on my elbow; his grip was hard and firm. We turned left along a corridor at the top of the stairs. The place was panelled in dark oak and looked as big as a museum. The pictures were mostly portraits in oils, in the style of the Spanish school. There was nobody else about and the place was so quiet that a mouse coughing would have seemed like a commotion; our footsteps were muffled in the thick carpet.

Then I caught a peculiar panting noise; I thought for a moment that my guide suffered from asthma. Then I looked over my shoulder and saw one of the big Dobermanns. He was padding along in the rear, keeping pace with us. He looked friendly enough, with his tongue sticking out of his pink mouth. He looked like he could eat off your hand. Or your leg come to that.

Presently the gallery finished and my guide pressed me to the left. I opened another door which had a brass handle. The guide said something to the dog.

When I looked round again the beast had disappeared. We stepped through the door. The guide still kept a grip on my elbow.

We were now very high up. Light spilled in from huge windows facing over the tops of trees. We were on another gallery which ran round three sides of one of the biggest rooms I had ever been in. I could see the reflection of light on polished oak floors far below; that and the shapes of carpets and furniture set out like it was being seen in an aerial photograph. We started walking along the gallery towards the head of a staircase.

We got almost to the head of the stairs when the man behind me suddenly tightened his grip on my arm. He dragged me to a halt. At the same moment there was a vibrating hum and something silvery-metallic in the half-light split the air in front of my face. There was a sharp, whining thud as a steel bolt about two feet long buried itself with an angry detonation in the wall about six feet in front of us.

'What the hell . . . ' I started to say,

twisting myself out of the guide's grasp.

There was a loud laugh from the floor of the great room.

'My apologies, gentlemen.'

I looked over the banister and took in a group of people around a table. But it was an old man sitting in a wheel-chair who arrested my attention. He had a glittering arc of metal in his hand, which he put down on the table.

'Please come in, sir, please come in,' he said.

We went on down the staircase.

# 8

## The Palisades

'William Tell, I presume?' I said.

The man in the wheel-chair gave another booming laugh.

'Come along in sir,' he said. 'You were in no danger, I can assure you. I am accurate to within less than half an inch.'

When I got up to him I could see he was an old man, well over seventy. His snow-white hair was plastered scantily over a great bare scalp that was all dents and angles. His eyes looked out at me from deep-chiselled caverns; iron grey eyebrows overhung his eye-sockets and white hair grew from his ears.

He had a deep yellow complexion and his big, heavy, old-fashioned mustache was brindled white and yellow; it gave him the look of an ancient hidalgo, which I had no doubt he was. He sat in the wheel-chair with a red and grey blanket covering his legs. He was dressed in an immaculate white shirt, buttoned at the neck and held in place by a grey silk stock from which a pearl-headed pin protruded. His sleeves were rolled back to his elbows, exposing forearms not emaciated as I should have expected, but knotted with hard muscle like wire ropes.

All the strength of his body seemed to have flown into his arms, as if to make up for his crippled legs. Bright yellow eyes looked steadily out at me from the darkness of his brows; his mouth was red-lipped and firm under the heavy mustache. He seemed to diminish the other people around him. All the life in the room was centred on his chair.

'General Diaz?' I said for form's sake, though the query seemed pretty superfluous.

'The same, sir,' he said. 'And you would be Mr Faraday?'

'I nodded.

'Please sit down, Mr Faraday,' he said in the same courteous manner. 'If you will excuse me for one moment. Captain Rodriguez . . .'

The man who had escorted me in snapped to attention and clicked his heels on the parquet floor. I dropped on to a leather-padded divan across from the old man's wheel-chair and studied the room as he and Rodriguez whispered together. It was all of a hundred feet long; at the back, way up the balcony along which we had come and to the left of the staircase was a large target whose concentric circles looked like a staring eye at that distance.

The single bolt he had fired from the steel bow which lay on the table at his side was buried accurately within the central disc of the bull. It was just slightly to the right of centre. Another Spanish-looking servant stood behind the old gentleman's chair; he carried in his hand a pair of heavy-duty pliers. Presently I saw him use them to retrieve the bolts; they must have been buried a couple of inches in the target. A canvas quiver was buckled to the side of the General's chair; it was three-quarters filled with the feathered flights of the steel-shafted bolts.

The bow itself was a formidable-looking weapon; I should have been hard put to bend it myself. It was an all-steel effort except for the binding of the grip. Even the cord was a thin steel cable. The General picked up the bow again as Captain Rodriguez saluted and hurried out. He took another of the servants with him. That left only the man standing behind the General's chair and a short, stocky fellow who had the look of a soldier. He had a revolver buckled around his waist too. He went and sat down in a chair at the side of the room where he could watch the proceedings.

The General took one of the steel bolts out of the quiver at his side and fitted it to the bow-string.

'Your indulgence, sir,' he said. 'I find that one soon gets out of practice. And one has few pleasures at my age. Archery has been a life-long interest.'

The General flexed the bow and sighted the bolt on the target; he had drawn on thick leather gloves. The muscles in his forearm swelled as he pulled the taut cable effortlessly back.

There was a deep organ note as the bolt left the bow, a noise like tearing calico and the same thrushing thud I had heard before. The bolt hummed like an angry wasp as it embedded itself. The feather head of the shaft made an indistinguishable pattern with the first one, the two bolts were so close. The aide at the side of the room clapped politely.

I watched the General fire three more; all were grouped within half an inch of the centre of the bull but the way he clicked his tongue you would have thought he had missed the target altogether. His eyes smouldered as he threw the bow down on the table in disgust and motioned the servant to collect the missiles.

'A lamentable exhibition, sir,' he said. 'I must apologize for such poor marksmanship. You will join me in a drink, I trust?'

He pressed a button at the side of his chair and a powerful electric motor hummed; the chair turned in a smooth circle and started rolling towards the great windows at the front of the vast room. I got up and kept pace with him down the carpet. He stopped in front of an impressive liquor cabinet; it seemed to contain every type of beverage known to man.

The General gave another rumbling laugh. 'My only weakness,' he said. 'Your pleasure, sir?'

'Scotch,' I said.

The General's chair whirred again as he angled it closer to the sideboard; there was a low serving surface, evidently designed specially for his needs, and he busied himself with glasses and a bowl of ice. The servant had gone up to the balcony to retrieve the arrows and the aide was reading a paper way down the room. I walked over to the window which must have been all of twenty feet across. I could see the grounds laid out like a relief map, with the drive crossing and re-crossing to the lodge; then the thin thread of the road and, above the far trees the top storeys of the country club.

The rubber-tyred wheel-chair squeaked on bare boards as I turned. The General put the generous-sized glass into my hand.

'To your health, sir,' he said, lifting his daiquiri.

I took one sip and then another, with increasing appreciation.

The General sat back in the chair, put down the glass on a small tray attachment he swung out from the arm, folded his long yellow hands and surveyed me. His eyes, under the profuse brows, were not unhumorous.

'You must be wondering, Mr Faraday, why an old cripple like myself is surrounded by such elaborate security arrangements. You see before you, sir, the remnants of a once considerable physique. To put it plainly, wounds caused by bomb fragments plus the encroachments of anno domini have made my legs something less than what they were. Hence the chair and all the other arrangements to flatter my ailment. But what the Almighty takes away in one direction he usually compensates in others and so it has been with me. The strength of my arms, which I have been at some pains to develop, and my sharpness of eye, remain undiminished, I am glad to

149

say. And there are days when I am even able to walk a few steps, albeit somewhat painfully.'

I started to speak but he held up his hand as if to call for patience. I went and sat in a carved wooden armchair of Spanish mahogany, put my drink on the General's leather-topped desk, and pulled the chair round to face him. He took another sip at his long glass before continuing.

'However, that is enough of my history,' he said. 'The matter in hand. You are, as I understand it, Mr Faraday, a private investigator? It would be superfluous to ask what sort of assignments you undertake?'

I grinned. 'The dangerous ones,' I said.

The General smiled a melancholy smile. 'Quite so,' he said. 'I fancied I recognized a kindred spirit.'

'I'd like to ask you a few questions, General,' I said. 'Principally about Miss Benson, though I am interested academically in Mr Holgren. I expect you heard I found both of them?'

General Diaz slowly inclined his head.

He held his daiquiri up to the light and squinted at the frozen contents of his glass. Beads of moisture glinted in the cold winter light.

'I had heard it suggested,' he said drily. 'We will leave over the small matter of trespassing in my grounds for the moment. I take it you are not implying that I had anything to do with either? Mr Holgren was a very valued friend and colleague of mine.'

'I didn't suggest anything, General,' I said evenly. 'But you can see how it looks to an outsider.'

He tapped with thin fingers on his glass; the noise made tiny shivering tinkles in the silence.

'I can indeed,' he said softly. 'You are retained by whom?'

'The employers of the dead girl,' I said. 'So far as they know — as far as anyone knows, apart from a handful of us — it's still a case for Missing Persons.'

The General stroked his long mustache; he sat hunched in his chair for so long that I thought he had gone to sleep. Except that his yellow eyes were fixed unwaveringly over my head and out through the window to the far hills.

'I am inclined to trust you, Mr Faraday,' he said, 'but I can say little without sanction from Sheriff Clark. He has not chosen to give that sanction for the moment. And until he does . . .'

He spread his arms wide on the blanket which enveloped his legs. He held up his hand again as if to ward off any further interruption on my part.

'Just let me say this, Mr Faraday. Do I look like a man who would liquidate his own lawyer in such a brutal manner? Or cut short the life of an innocent young girl in my own grounds? Let me suggest to you that you reorientate your line of reasoning. Precautions which may seem to you to be directed towards keeping people in, may equally well be designed to keep them out.'

He stopped again while his eyes travelled blindly round the great room. The rustle of the aide's paper as he turned over a page sounded loud in the silence of the winter afternoon.

'I had already got that far,' I said. 'That

is, shortly after I met you.'

General Diaz turned his eyes directly at me now and he was smiling. 'Diaz is not my real name, Mr Faraday,' he said. 'It would not take you long to find out the truth. A search through old newspaper files in any decent public library would do the trick. I choose to bury myself in this small place because it suits me. I was once Chief of Police under one of the former regimes in Cuba. I have always been a just man. But certain things were necessary at particular times. I am a man with many enemies. More I cannot say at the moment.'

He shrugged and reached out for the glass again.

'I am an old man. I have no fear of death. But many people depend upon me for their livelihood. For that reason and that reason alone I would like to go on in peace and quietness for another few years.'

His eyes closed and he sank back in the chair. He held out his hand for me to shake.

'And now, if you do not mind, Mr

Faraday, I should like to rest. I usually have a short sleep in the afternoon. If you co-operate with Sheriff Clark I am sure that he will keep you fully informed.'

'Surely,' I said. I got up, finished off my drink and stood looking down at him as he sat in the chair.

'It seems to me that you have as much right as anyone to know what this is all about, Mr Faraday,' he said.

His voice sharpened and he caught at my arm. 'And it is of vital importance that you take heed of the Sheriff's advice. For your own protection as much as for the sake of anyone else.'

He pressed the switch of his wheelchair control; the motor whirred and the chair started moving slowly down the room. I kept pace beside it again. The Spanish servant reappeared at the stairhead and came down towards us. The aide got up and came over towards the chair. He stood with his hand on the butt of his gun.

General Diaz looked up at me. 'Incidentally, sir, that was splendidly done, that business with the dog. I saw something of it through my night-glasses. You are a man of commendable nerve and initiative. But you forgot one thing. A wise General always leaves one unguarded gap in his defences, through which the enemy may be lured in.'

His eyes twinkled and he laughed again.

'Think nothing of it, sir. No harm done. Though if you had been an enemy, things would have ended very differently.'

We shook hands again. 'Goodbye, sir,' I said. 'I hope we meet again soon.'

His grip was still crushing my fingers as I went up the stairs. The General went to another staircase at the other side of the room. The aide clipped his wheel-chair to a girdered ramp at the side of the stairs. More motors whirred and the General kept pace with me as his own lift brought him up to my level.

The Spanish servant led me out along the balcony and down the way I had come in. I was surprised to see the time by my wristlet watch when I reached the main hall. I had only been half an hour with the old boy but it had seemed like a couple of decades at least.

'Good afternoon, sir,' said the guide politely as he let me out. I went down the steps to my car. The guard with the Dobermann was standing about a hundred yards off down the driveway. He waved to me in a friendly fashion. I got in the car, sat for a moment or two and lit a cigarette. I felt I needed a little time to get back into the world again.

Then I switched on the ignition, let in the clutch and glided back down the drive. I waited at the main lodge gate while the guard unlocked it; his companion had to phone up the house again to make sure it was all right.

I drove slowly out from The Palisades main entrance and turned left back to town. It wasn't until then that I saw Clark's police car parked almost opposite. He hooted. I stopped the Buick, switched off and went over towards him. He sat smoking and watched me come.

# 9

## Two-Handed Showdown

Clark held the door open for me. I got in and sat beside him. 'Satisfied?' he said quietly.

I turned to face him in the narrow confines of the front passenger seat.

'That General Diaz had nothing to do with the two kills, yes,' I said.

'I asked you to leave the General alone,' he said mildly. 'He saw me anyway,' I answered.

'Only on my O.K.,' said Clark. 'Who did you think the lodge-keeper was ringing before he let you in? Woodrow Wilson? If I hadn't given the word you'd still be dusting the seat of your pants outside the gates right now.'

'So the two of you work together,' I said. 'But let's get one thing straight. We're both on the same side?'

Clark didn't reply at once. Then he got

out his old briar, started filling it. He grinned suddenly.

'It's time we levelled,' he said. 'Shall I begin or will you?'

'I think we got two different things here,' I said. 'Leaving aside Holgren for the moment, the Benson girl's death was an accident. For some reason or other she was on top of Diaz' wall and stopped a bullet meant for the General. There's a guest house opposite; from the front windows there's a direct line-up with the big room on the top floor of The Palisades. Anyone with a high-powered rifle could have picked off the old boy; anyone with a grudge, that is. But the top of the wall's in the line of fire. If the girl had been on the wall, she could have got between at the critical moment. Sounds crazy, I know . . . '

Clark sat with his eyes closed, puffing at his pipe. 'Go on,' he said. 'Doc says the girl's got bruising, like she fell from a height. It adds up.'

'I went out here to the guest house this morning,' I said. 'In Room fifty-nine I found the dressing table had been moved from the window, maybe to give a better sight for the trigger boy. There were traces of powder burns on the window frame.'

Clark sat up straight with his eyes wide open.

'You were going to report this, of course?'

'It was only a hunch,' I said. 'But there was so much holding-out going on from your side that I figured you probably knew already.'

Clark grinned again. 'Go on,' he said. 'Any more conclusions?'

I shook my head. 'I didn't pump the old lady at the guest house but she could probably describe the guests, even at this distance in time. She struck me as being that type. It might give you something to go on.'

Clark rubbed his hands. 'You done well, Mr Faraday. Real well. And we'll overlook some of the little peculiarities of your methods. Like getting over people's walls. Or forgetting to report things. A P.I. can stick his neck out where we run up against red tape. I think you got something important here. And I won't forget it. Now I'm goin' to be equally frank.'

He tapped his pipe into the car ash tray and looked across at the lodge gates of The Palisades.

'You were all wrong about the General, son, though I don't blame you for having suspicions. He's just about the best friend this town ever had. A school, health clinic hospital annexe — you name it, the General's had a hand in it. He's always got his fist in his pocket, especially when it comes to the young people. That's why your suspicions were so durn'd ridiculous. Only I couldn't come right out in the open, partly because I promised him and partly because the whole thing sounds so fantastic.'

'I'm listening,' I said.

He drummed with one hand on the wheel of the car.

'The General was a very big man in the country he came from,' he said. 'Where'd he tell you?'

'Cuba,' I said.

'Well, it wasn't really Cuba,' said Clark, 'but it'll do. It was one of those places

160

where they have a firing squad one minute and a brand new government the next. The General always makes out he was Chief of Police in Havana. In fact he was Minister of Justice — the biggest man in the Government, next to the President. Quite a few years ago now there was an attempted coup. The man behind it was the President's biggest rival. The coup failed. Diaz conducted the prosecutions in person and the leader was executed. The others in the conspiracy, including the executed leader's brother, got prison sentences ranging from fifteen to twenty-five years.'

Clark paused again and started to re-light his pipe. I wound down the window on my side to get some fresh air in.

'This is where it starts to get tricky,' said Clark. 'In the course of time the General retired and came to the States to live. He brought with him some of his supporters, ex-officers and the like, all of whom were personal friends. These, together with his body servants, made up the household at The Palisades.

Because, like you've guessed, Esteban's brother — that was the dead leader's name — had sworn to get Diaz, and they've got long memories in those parts. Last year there was an amnesty and all the survivors of the coup were released from prison. They included Hernando and several fanatical supporters. A few months ago we got word that four of them had landed in the States.'

Clark puffed on the pipe, causing it to belch smoke and sparks. His face looked angry in the glow.

'We got the Government to keep tabs on 'em, of course, as far as possible, but it's a difficult job in a big country like ours. They didn't know where the General was, but then neither did we know where they were after a bit, because all four disappeared after they'd been traced to New York. In the meantime I advised the General to step up his security arrangements. This is about where we were until Holgren got it.'

He paused and then went on, 'Now does anything strike you in particular about Holgren's death? The reason, I mean?'

'A finger man?' I said. 'Supposing someone in town had located Diaz. Or the Cubans had turned up somewhere? And Holgren had spotted them. And come up to Mudville to warn the General?'

Clark assented gloomily.

'It doesn't fit very well,' I said. 'Why wouldn't he have phoned him instead of driving all the way up here on a wet, cold night?'

Clark smiled slowly. 'We know the reason for that. The General was way on the other side of the County. And maybe it was something Holgren couldn't talk about on the phone. It's a small exchange here too, remember.'

'It all figures,' I said, 'except for the girl and that sounds pretty way-out.'

'That one is tough,' said Clark, 'but it'll fall into place. So she was running along the wall and got hit in the side. You'd better get with Cheney quick before I haul him in.'

'He's next on my list,' I said. I sat and

finished my cigarette. 'Several Cubans,' I said. 'Wouldn't they be kinda conspicuous in a small place like this?'

Clark shook his head. 'Not particularly. You know as well as I do, California's full of Spanish-speaking nationals. The Mudville finger-man is what I'm concentrating on.'

Another thought had occurred to me as we had been speaking.

'Then it was you who hit me over the head out at the Diaz place,' I said, fingering the bump. Clark turned red and coughed heavily. Then he joined me busting out laughing.

'Afraid you asked for it, Faraday. But I didn't know who the hell it was when you came out of there. You were lucky I didn't plug you.'

'It would have been difficult lying flat on your back,' I said mildly. 'I didn't have time for niceties.'

'To be honest,' said Clark, 'I was winded and when I got up I started running in the opposite direction to where you must have been lying. I'd been called out to the General's that night for our usual weekly chat. We mull over the security arrangements and so forth. Then things started popping.'

'O.K. Sheriff,' I said. 'I shouldn't have been there, as you said. But it only increased my suspicions when you didn't speak up after I told you about it.'

I got out of the car and stood by the window. Clark got out the other side.

'What's the next move?' I said.

'I'll go check the country club,' he said. 'I might get a decent description. If you can fit in Cheney and the Bensons later today, I can release the news of the girl's death tonight. The Cheney lad may not be directly involved but ten to one he was with her when she got it. Give me a ring. You and me and the General ought to have a long talk in the next twenty-four hours.'

'Right,' I said. I started walking towards the Buick.

'And Faraday . . . ', Clark called. I turned round.

'Many thanks again,' he said with a smile. He went on towards the country club. I got in my car and drove back to town.

I pulled up at the side of Redbarn Autos and parked the car. I walked back down to the Post Office and called Stella.

'Well, well,' she said. 'Another country heard from.'

'Never mind the comedy,' I said. 'Listen good, honey. I haven't got too many nickels.'

'That's more like you, Mike,' she said. 'Always counting the pennies.'

I ignored that too. I put her in the picture. I could hear her pen scratching over the paper as I spoke. I had to put some more money in the coin-slot after that.

'This is confidential,' I told Stella. 'Nothing's to leak out, least of all to Dame Dora, until you get my sayso. Clark can't sit on it later than tonight so it should be in the L.A. papers come tomorrow morning.'

I arranged with her that she would ring Dame Dora at her home that evening; we made it around nine. That way the call would beat the regular ten p.m. radio and

TV news bulletins. I didn't think Clark would make any announcement before nine.

'How did you make out with Patti Morgan?' I asked Stella.

'I've been doing my homework,' she said. 'She's in the clear so far as I can make out. Impeccable background, as they say. Before you ring off, I got some more dope on Holgren.'

'Hold it,' I told her. I went out the booth and over to the main counter; the woman behind it gave me change for a dollar. I got back to the phone as the time signal started buzzing again. I fed the coin-box.

'You were saying?' I said.

'Holgren,' said Stella. 'He was in practice in Latin America years ago. That's where he met the General. Only Diaz wasn't his real name.'

'I know,' I told her. 'Where did you get all this stuff?'

'Down at the Library,' she said. 'I had to go a long way back in the files.'

'Good girl,' I said and meant it.

'Thanks, boss,' she said. 'You likely to

be making it back before Christmas?'

'I might just get lucky,' I said.

'Take care, Mike,' she said. 'Miss you.'

She rang off without waiting for me to say goodbye and left me looking at something rude someone had carved with a penknife on the wall of the booth. I came out so pensive I almost left my change on the top of the phone-book cabinet. But not quite. A horn hooted as I got outside. A white roadster drifted down the street; a golden dazzle of hair showed behind the wheel. Patti Morgan waved and smiled as she cruised by.

An old guy with buck teeth and gold-rimmed pince-nez looked after her like the wave had been for him, then shot me an envious glance.

'She's got something,' he said to me admiringly.

'And she's hanging on to it, too,' I told him and went on down the street.

I walked round the side of Redbarn Autos. A tall attendant with a fat belly and blond hair was tapping one of the gasoline pumps and frowning at the dial.

'Mr Cheney about?' I said.

He jerked his thumb towards the main building. 'He's not in the showroom,' he said. 'Try the apartment. I thought I saw him go up a while ago.'

This suited me. Besides, it would avoid the joker with the dead ferret under his nose. I walked along past the showroom and up a flight of steps flanked by a blue-painted iron railing. I pushed the buzzer on a door set back behind potted shrubs; that was painted blue too. I heard the faraway noise of the buzzer but no-one came to the door. As I pushed it again I found it was ajar. I walked on through into a kitchen. It was a big apartment with a large ice-chest on one side and pressed steel sink units.

A man was slumped at a table with his head resting on his hands. A bottle and an empty glass sat on the table in front of him. He didn't stir so I put a hand on his shoulder. He still didn't move so I shook him. He turned a bleared face towards me.

'It's Faraday,' I said. 'You know why I've come?'

He passed shaking fingers over his face.

169

The film over his eyes cleared.

'We found her,' I told him. 'Buried under the tree. You ready to talk now?'

His face turned yellow as the sense of my words began to penetrate. He went over unsteadily towards the sink and began to vomit. He turned on the tap and sluiced his face in the running water. I went and took a towel off a hook on the kitchen door and threw it to him. He caught it and started to mop his face.

'Thanks,' he said. He looked better now though his eyes were red-rimmed and bloodshot. He went and sat back at the table. I got another chair and sat opposite him. He took the cigarette I offered him from my pack. I held the flame of a match to the tip of his cigarette. It took him three attempts to get it lit.

'You were there?' I said.

He drew in the smoke. 'Yes,' he said slowly. He feathered out the smoke in a long, shuddering sigh.

'You'll have to talk about it,' I said. 'But if you go see Clark voluntarily things will be a lot easier for you.'

He nodded again. 'I was there. I'll tell you all about it.'

* ★ ★ ★

'What the hell was she doing on top of the wall?' I said. Cheney drank his second cup of coffee and put down the cup heavily. 'I can see it was stupid keeping quiet about it,' he said, 'but there's been a lot of trouble with Carmen's parents. And my own father told me to keep my mouth shut. I knew it wouldn't be any good. These last weeks have been hell.'

'Just take it slow and tell it from the beginning,' I said. Cheney tapped the cup on the saucer in front of him; the chink sounded very loud in the silence of the kitchen. There was only the faint rapping of rain again on the windows.

'You were right in your guess, Mr Faraday,' he said in a dead voice. 'Carmen and me did meet that Saturday. We were pretty fond of one another. But things were against us from the beginning. Carmen's father hated my old man and he was prejudiced from way back. I never pretended to be a saint but I was sincere about her. And my old man wouldn't wear it either. He's a hard case and he gave me a rough time. What with one thing and another we had to keep our meetings under wraps. The only real friend we had was Carmen's mother, but she's not a strong character when it comes to standing up to Mr Benson.'

'We met,' I said. 'I see what you mean.'

I waited for him to go on. He lit another cigarette with nervous fingers but some of the colour was coming back into his face.

'I picked Carmen up in my car that afternoon,' he went on. 'We had a place where we met way out of town, where it was quiet and secluded. There's very few people out there in winter-time anyway. She'd told her mother she was taking in a movie with a girl friend. We rode around and then I parked near The Palisades. We were necking for a bit . . . '

He stopped momentarily.

'You can skip that part,' I said. 'I was young once myself.'

'Well, Mr Faraday,' Cheney said,

'Carmen was always a wild type of girl. Not wild in the bad sense, you understand. You wouldn't realize it to look at her, but she had a streak of crazy good humour in her. We'd been sitting there for a while and she said she'd always wanted to see inside the old General's grounds. He's been rather a mystery man around town and there were all sorts of stories about his household, his bodyguard, and lately the dogs.'

'So you decided to have a look inside,' I said.

He drew hard on the cigarette. 'Carmen did,' he said. 'I wasn't very keen, but I didn't want to chicken out in front of a girl. I parked the car way up the road out of sight. There was no-one about and we walked along the wall and after a bit found a gap and climbed into the grounds.'

He paused again and sat staring in front of him for so long that I figured he'd forgotten my presence. The thin fingers of rain kept tapping at the kitchen window.

'Well, sir, we had a look around. It was all rather disappointing, really, and damned uninviting on a winter afternoon. We stayed for about ten minutes or so, chasing one another about, generally horsing around, you know the sort of thing. Then I was all for getting on out. We hadn't made any noise or anything, but I always had the dogs at the back of my mind. But that wouldn't do for Carmen. She had to fetch a ladder and climb up on top of the wall.'

He paused again and drew on the cigarette; a fire engine went by in the distance, its siren muffled in the rain. We waited until the high whine died, chopped off by the edges of the buildings.

'Anyway, she had this crazy idea. She started to run across the top of the wall. She was laughing, the wind blowing in her hair and calling that she could beat me. I started to run to keep pace with her. Then she called out and fell off the wall. I ran back. I didn't know what happened. I thought she was fooling at first. She was that sort of girl.'

'You found she'd been shot?' I said quietly.

Cheney nodded. 'I was stunned. She

didn't move or call out again. There was blood all over the place. I thought at first she'd cut herself in falling. When I understood I figured she'd been shot by someone on the General's staff. The word's out all over town about their security precautions. Then I became confused and afraid. There was nothing I could do for Carmen; I thought of her parents and my own father and all the trouble there'd be.'

'So you panicked?' I said.

'I completely lost my head. I dragged her body over under the tree and covered it up with grass and bits of stick. Then I got the hell out as quickly as I could. I put the ladder back first and got away from the Diaz place the way we'd come in. Nobody saw me as far as I knew. I drove back to town. I was dead certain I hadn't been spotted. That's why I was so rattled when you said there'd been a witness. Though I knew it would come out in the end.'

He got up and went over to the sink and turned the tap on to his cigarette butt; he washed it down the sink and came back to the table.

'I might have come out with it sooner,' he said. 'I lied to Sheriff Clark but I intended to see you after our talk at the pool hall. Except that my old man had found out. I came in pretty high one night and said a few things I shouldn't. He wormed the story out of me; he said it was best to leave everything where it was. He threatened to tan the hide off me if I said anything.'

'Did he?' I said.

'Believe me, Mr Faraday, I wanted to go to the police long ago, but I'd left it too late,' he said. 'What could I tell the Sheriff that wouldn't leave me seriously implicated?'

'You're still seriously implicated,' I told him. 'And surely you had a duty to Carmen? For all we know this long delay may have made it impossible to trace the killer. All you've done is involve yourself in a heap of trouble.'

Cheney turned his haggard face towards me. He let his breath out in another long sigh. 'Let's get it over with,' he said. 'I'm ready any time you are.'

'Ready for what, Newton?' said a sneering voice from the door. The big man I'd met in the showroom was standing in the kitchen doorway. He just about filled it. I hadn't heard him come up the stairway because of the low hiss of falling rain. But here he was, life-sized and twice as nasty. The dead ferret under his nose twitched and his little pig-eyes glinted meanly. He looked like he'd been drinking. Guess it ran in the family.

Cheney turned to me.. 'This is my father,' he said as though apologizing.

'I'm sorry about that,' I told him. If I was trying to rile the old man up I certainly succeeded. The information had come as quite a surprise. The senior Cheney ignored me.

'What's this snooper doing here?' he asked in a nasty voice.

'I always drop in for a game of checkers about this time,' I said pleasantly. 'Your son's got the makings of a first-class player. And it enlivens these wet winter evenings.'

'What's going on here?' said Cheney thickly. His son got up unsteadily from

**177**

the table. He blinked helplessly at me. He kept his face away from his father.

He swallowed once or twice and then managed to get out, 'I'm sorry, dad. I got to do the right thing.'

'Like hell you will,' the big man screamed. He came into the room and kicked the door shut behind him. He waddled over towards me. Close up, he looked meaner and more repellent than ever. His fists were balled under the cuffs of his smart blue suit. Crimson patches showed on his thick jowls.

'Just stand aside, Mr Cheney,' I said quietly. 'Your son's got a date with Sheriff Clark.'

'No-one's leaving this room,' he said with a suppressed growl of rage.

'Don't be stupid, dad,' said the son with more spirit than I gave him credit for. 'You know I got to go with Mr Faraday.'

'Only one place this cheap shamus is going,' the big man said. He was standing with his back half turned to me, speaking to his son. So I didn't see till too late his clenched fist travelling up from his side at tremendous speed. Heavy with rings it came in a fast back-hander and caught me a glancing blow on the angle of the jaw. The kitchen spun on its axis and I tasted blood. A blackjack appeared in Cheney's hand as if it had suddenly grown there; it whistled in the air. Newton Cheney fell against the wall as the kitchen table went over with a clatter. Bottles splintered on the tiled floor; I went in under the older Cheney's flailing arm and put my fist into his belly, right up past the wrist, with all my strength.

He was like a bowl of mush here; the breath went out of his lungs, he gagged and his face turned green. The blackjack fell down on to the floor among the bottles. The side of his boot caught me in the groin but by then I had got my two clenched hands down on the bridge of his nose. His eyes glazed and blood spurted from his nostrils. He went down with a crash in the debris. He moaned once or twice but didn't get up again. I hobbled to the wall and propped myself up. I fought for breath as Cheney went over and lifted his father.

'I'm sorry I had to do that,' I said.

'He asked for it,' he said in a voice which sounded like he was enjoying it. The big man groaned again. Young Cheney went over to the sink and filled a bowl with cold water. He came back and slopped it in handfuls over his father's face. The older Cheney swallowed water; his eyes opened. He blinked once or twice, then started to retch. Cheney helped his father up. I picked up the overturned table and a chair. Cheney set his father down on the chair. It seemed like a good time to be moving.

'He'll get over it,' I said. 'See you around.'

I went out and closed the door behind me. The rain felt good on my face. I went down the steps and along the road to my car. The water had drifted in through the leaky hood on to the front seat again. I sponged it off. I was just going to close the door when I heard running feet. Newton Cheney put his head in at the passenger door. He looked better than I'd seen him.

'Let's go,' he said.

I drove quickly through town to the Benson place. If there was one spot I'd rather not be this afternoon this was it. But I'd told Clark. Young Cheney got out of the car and joined me in front of the fence. His face looked like wet putty. I put my hand on his shoulder.

'Let me do the talking,' I said.

We went slowly up the drive to the house. Mrs Benson was opening the front door before we got there.

# 10

## How Lucky Can You Get?

It was still only a quarter to nine when I got to Greenside Manor. I stopped at the end of the road and lit a cigarette. The thin rain whispered monotonously on the canvas roof of the Buick. It seemed like it had ever since this case began. They were still going over Cheney's statement for the fifth time at Clark's office when I left. I glanced at my watch again. The papers would have a carnival come the morning. I'd asked Clark to play my part down. I shouldn't get much rest at the Pinetop otherwise.

When I finished the cigarette it was just on nine. I put in the gear and cruised on down the road. The house I wanted was a large bungalow set back among lawns and dark bushes. It was a cul-de-sac and I reversed around in the road at the end, against a steep bank and came on back. I ran the Buick in up the concrete drive and into a big plastic car-port next to the white convertible Patti Morgan had been driving earlier that afternoon.

The bungalow was really a two-storey building, for the big-windowed rooms set into the dormer roof made another floor. There were pots and boxes set about the place, which had once contained flowering shrubs and plants; just now they were filled with what looked like pieces of blackened stick. A thin mist was coming up as I went along the main path to the house. It would have been worth a fortune to Bela Lugosi.

I got out of the rain under a natural pine porch held up by futuristic steel pins set into the concrete walk; the front windows were shrouded in Venetian blinds, but a faint pink glow came from behind them. It looked warm and welcoming in the darkness and dampness of the night. In back something dripped on to metal. It made a melancholy tinkle in the dusk. All the other houses round about sat back behind their box hedges and their clipped ornamental trees and minded their own business.

I pushed a brass button set into one of the pine porch uprights and listened to a carillon play from far away. A lantern blinked in the roof above my head and lit up the porch and a four yard strip of lawn. I stood and studied the pebble glass set in the panes of the porch door. A shadow moved behind the layers of glass and the inner door opened. I could see it was Patti Morgan even at that distance. I held my box of candy and waited for her to open the main door.

'Right on time,' she said.

'I'm never late where food's involved,' I said.

She grinned. 'I can see you're a born flatterer. Come on in.'

She looked a treat. She had on a severely tailored blue skirt which set off her figure in a way that should have legislation against it. High-heeled black velvet shoes emphasized her height. Her pale blue tailored shirt with the darker blue stripe re-echoed the skirt; she wore a plain gold circlet on her left wrist. Her hair shimmered and reflected the light as the porch bulbs caught the heavy buttercup-yellow mass.

I shut the outer door and heard it lock behind me. She flipped a switch as we went through and the porch light died. She locked the inner door after us too. The hall was all in biscuit brown, including the carpets; nothing broke the overall tone of the walls except for the series of pastels in heavy white frames which seemed to float out at you. The effect was effortless; but it denoted a lot of taste and a lot of money.

Two crystal chandeliers hung against the dark grey ceiling of the hall. Patti Morgan walked me through into a living room which was as light as the hall had been discreet. The walls were pale, the carpet olive green. A few Swedish paper-shaded lamps were dotted about. The furniture was frail-looking but very solid Scandinavian of a light gold colour. The drapes at the French windows and the cushions and fittings of the divans were olive green too.

She smiled, giving me another view of those fine teeth. 'I brought these for your mother,' I said, giving her the box of candy.

'Thanks, Mike.' Her surprise was genuine. Then she covered her face with her cupped hands. A suppressed gurgle of laughter came out. I looked at her inquiringly.

'No mother?' I said. She nodded helplessly.

'That means no father, either,' I said.

She nodded again. I sat on one of the divans and put down my other packages. 'Not that I'm complaining,' I said, 'But you did say you came up here just to see them.'

She had control of herself now. She smoothed down her skirt as she sat in a high-backed chair opposite me.

'I forgot all about it this morning. They had to go up to Maine for a week to see relatives. But how sweet of you to think of mother. Do you think we might open them? They look delicious.'

A pink tongue protruded from her mouth as she tried the cellophane wrapping over the red silk bow on the box.

186

'What mother doesn't know about she won't worry over,' I said.

'A very good maxim,' she said. 'But you'd better take your coat off. I'm afraid I'm not being a very good hostess.'

I took off my raincoat and she carried it outside to the hall.

'Get yourself a drink,' she called through the doorway. 'There's Scotch on the sideboard.'

I went over and started fiddling around among the glasses. I found a bottle of Old Kentucky on top of the sideboard and some nice crystal glasses in the cupboard. I poured out two generous slugs. The rain tapped at the windows with light brushing movements. Patti Morgan came back through into the living room dusting her hands.

'Sorry, no ice here. We'll have to go out in the kitchen. What have we here?'

'Rich gifts from the Orient,' I said.

'Oh, Mike, you shouldn't,' she said, but I could see from the way her eyes sparkled that she liked it. It was only some odds and ends of fruit that I'd picked up on the way over; some out of season strawberries, asparagus tips, a bunch or two of grapes. She bit into one of the big blue grapes with very white teeth.

'Delicious, Mike,' she said. 'You mustn't spoil me.'

'I always carry a pound of grapes for instant orgies,' I told her.

She pulled at my ear with slim, well-manicured fingers.

'The kitchen, chum,' she said. 'Bring the glasses.'

I looked around the room, contrasted the warmth and light and comfort with the conditions of the last few days, fingered the slight bump on my cheek, looked after Patti Morgan's retreating nylons and followed her quickly into the kitchen. I'd never had it so good.

★ ★ ★

The kitchen was about two blocks long and only slightly less palatial than the Orchid Room on the United States. About halfway down, the working area turned into a dining-room with teak

188

furniture, recessed lighting, sporting prints and expensive hand-painted plates clipped to the walls. At the very far end near the window was a large bar made of oiled teak. It had high stools with leather seats, like a genuine cocktail lounge.

Patti Morgan went over to a sink-unit that looked like the engine room of the U.S.S. Lexington and started washing the fruit. Copper-bottomed fry pans came in different sizes down the room, slung from hooks under the big, natural-grain wood cupboards.

'Just ice, no water,' she said, playing with stainless steel taps. I went over to the bar and around behind the glass-topped counter. Presently I found a large ice-chest disguised as a wooden shelf unit. I prized some cubes loose with what looked like a solid silver pick, put two cubes in each glass and carried the drinks down towards Patti. She'd put on a small white apron and was looking highly professional. She had all sorts of stuff laid out on top of one of the working surfaces. Pleasant aromas were making hints from the depths of the oven.

I handed her a glass and went and sat down on a combination ladder-stool over near the sink, where I could see what she was doing. She was making like busy with a small knife in one hand while she kept an eye on several things on the stove-top.

'I didn't know it was going to be an eight-course effort or I'd have worn my tuxedo,' I said.

She turned a flushed face to me. 'Just simple living. They looking after you down at the Pinetop?'

'Tolerable,' I said. 'But tonight I can see the drawbacks.'

Patti Morgan paused in stirring something in one of the pans. 'Mother and Dad worked hard for all this,' she said. 'I enjoy it week-ends. But you ought to see the place I live in at L.A. Modest isn't the word.'

'It's a date,' I said.

I got up and went over and took my drink into the dining area. I sat down with my back to the wall where I could see her through the teak-slatted room divider. I lit a cigarette, sipped at my

190

Scotch and listened to the faint tapping of rain. A snatch of Johnny Hodges came through on a hidden speaker as she flipped a radio switch. Patti came over with her drink and sat down across from me.

'Can I help with anything?' I asked.

She laughed. 'I can't imagine it.'

'I fry a mean egg,' I said.

She sipped at her Scotch. 'How old would you be?' she asked.

'About twenty-one and engaged to Brigette Bardot if I had any sense,' I said.

She laughed. 'That's put me in my place.'

'I'm a good eight years older than you, if you really want to know,' I said.

She pondered. 'Just about the right age.'

I thought the conversation was getting a bit dangerous so I got up and wandered back into the kitchen. By the time we'd carried the stuff in, and I'd started on my second Scotch I'd forgotten the night, the rain and the mist.

★ ★ ★

The food was good, best I'd tasted in a long while. Though I'm no connoisseur, Patti Morgan knew how to cook. We started with iced melon, dusted with the finest sieved sugar. The steak had been cooked in wine and was just how I liked it. She'd dug up a good Beaujolais to go with the meat too. Somehow I'd been expecting a Californian-type riesling. It was so unlooked-for I almost choked.

After the green salad I gave up wondering and just concentrated on the cooking. She'd lit a couple of small red candles in the alcove where we sat and doused the lamps at this end of the room. The candlelight came and went so that the image of her face faded and grew and faded again in the fluttering light. It suited her. The only sound in the room was the occasional clink of china as she gathered up the plates, took them down to the work area and re-appeared with the next course.

The faint presence of the rain at the windows was unnoticed now. She served real coffee, hot, strong and black as jet, the way you almost never get it in this

192

country. Europe's about the only place you can get decent coffee, but she'd studied it. I wondered where. She was beginning to reveal unsuspected qualities. Her eyes were quiet, amused as she lit a cigarette at the candle flame. The cloying taste of the Chartreuse had no sooner been superseded by the coffee, than she poured the brandy into the big balloon glasses. We drank silently, appreciatively.

'I won't insult you by saying that was great,' I said after a long silence. 'But you know what I mean.'

She put her hand on my arm; it rested there just that bit longer than necessary. I knew that signal well.

'We'll leave the dishes till later,' she said. 'Come on over to the bar.'

I went over and sat down on one of the high stools. She put on a shaded lamp behind the bar which gave a pink rinse to all the bottles. Either it was that or the drinks had been stronger than I thought. Not that the tinting was bad. I had gotten into that sort of mood by now. Patti fiddled about behind the bar and came up with a bowl of ice from the big chest.

The radio was playing something by Ellington now; something blue, high and slightly offkey. Perhaps it wasn't but it had that effect.

Patti came and sat on the stool next to me like we were at the bar of a downtown hotel. I sat and looked at the pink lighting of the bar and enjoyed the warmth of the brandy which was moving slowly up from my stomach to envelope the rest of my body as far as the ears and tried not to think of the way the situation was leading.

'Nickel for them?'

I turned round to face Patti on the stool at my side. Which was a mistake. I should have stayed where I was, sipped my drink, looked at the pink lighting and minded my own business. But I didn't. I turned round and there was her face, right up against mine. The pink light shone on the smooth contours of her hair, which fitted her face like a sculpted helmet. Her skirt was riding way up as she sat on the stool. She had a fantastic pair of stems on her. They were burning a hole in my eyeballs from where I was sitting. Hell, so I kissed her, not being

194

made of asbestos. This is where things started to get tricky.

'Mike,' she said, in a slow and vibrant voice that set me tingling all the way down to my arch supports. 'Do you have to go back tonight?'

'I can't stay any later than six in the morning,' I told her. 'My grandmother always warned me to get in before the milkman. It doesn't look good for a man's public relations image.'

She laughed. 'That's fine, then,' she said. 'We can take it nice and slow.'

'Seems to me you didn't entirely plan this as a casual operation,' I said.

She put a warm hand on my lips. 'Too true, chum,' she said. 'We have to move fast in this neck of the woods. Action, boy, not words.'

I tried to oblige.

★  ★  ★

The bedroom had white walls, a white bedspread, even a white telephone on the bedside table. So the black lace under-pants and minute black brassiere which was about all she was wearing at the moment, made a vivid contrast in the dim light of the one lamp we'd got switched on. Her skin was dark brown; unlike most natural blondes it took the sun well. The tan didn't come from sun-lamps either. You can always tell. I'd carried her in in rather a hurry as things turned out. She was already taking off her top clothes like she didn't want to wait.

'Don't spoil it,' I said. 'I usually like to do that myself.'

'Don't grumble, darling,' she said, biting my ear. 'I'll leave the rest for you.'

She kissed me again then. I got the point. Right now she was lying by my side, looking up at the ceiling. Her lips moved quietly like she was talking to herself, but maybe she was just counting the squares in the ceiling panels.

She had a fantastic figure; it's a funny thing about women, but you can never tell with clothes on. Girls that look about average are stunning when they're peeled and the terrific lookers are usually as flat-chested as the front of a filing cabinet. This evening was bonus night. I'd picked one who not only looked good in clothes but was terrific out of them. Or she'd picked me. Right now I didn't care who'd done what.

Patti's thighs rustled together as she shifted over on the bed toward me. There was the Sound of the Week if you like. It certainly sent my blood count up. She was still wearing shoes, stockings and her suspender belt. Patti Morgan must have sensed what I was thinking. She looked at me coolly, as though confident of her power.

'Sadist,' she said and nipped my ear again.

That was the detonator. She moaned once as we rolled over and our lips met. I shifted position and got to the lamp switch. The room went into darkness. Then I ripped the remainder of her clothes off and jumped on her.

She was whimpering. 'You can do anything you like, darling. Anything you like . . .'

'I intend to, baby,' I said.

I did.

# 11

## Encore for Ice-Picks

When I awoke it was around half-past four according to the luminous dial of my watch. I ran a finger along Patti's warm flank. She shivered and then nestled closer into my arms.

'Time to be moving, honey,' I said.

We kissed again. I put on the dim lamp and draped a handkerchief over the shade. It was always the worst part, scrabbling around for pants and pieces of gaily-discarded clothing on the morning after. Patti turned in the bed and watched with amusement. 'There's a shower through the far door,' she said.

I went into the bathroom, had a hot sluice and towelled myself. When I had dressed I went back into the bedroom. Patti wasn't in the bed. I walked through the lounge and into the kitchen. Hot, strong coffee bubbled in a percolator. She had brushed her hair and looked great, even at that hour of the morning, in a white towelling dressing gown. She handed me a cup; we sat back at the table in the alcove. When I got up to leave she clung to me like she was never going to let go.

'I leave town tomorrow night,' she said.

'I'll ring,' I said. 'Thanks for everything, honey. You're a great girl.'

I held her close and tight and warm to me the way a girl like her should be held. Then she pushed me away with a sigh.

'See you,' she said.

The night struck cold and wet and foggy as I got out the porch. The Buick was coated with globules of moisture and the windscreen streamed with water. The front door catch clicked ever so slightly behind me as I got up to the car. I found the usual pool of dampness on the driving seat. I sponged off the wet, cleared the windscreen and backed the car carefully down the drive.

I didn't switch on the lights or the engine. There was nothing but darkness and fog and wet all around me. When I got to the road she just failed to move, so I got out, pushed at the windscreen upright and ghosted her slowly down the road. When I was about five blocks away I put her in gear and drove back to the Pinetop. I hung up my trench coat in the hall. There were two envelopes lying inside the front door.

One was the buff-coloured flimsy of Western Union. I tore open the flap; the telegram was from Dame Dora. The last bit said; GET THOSE RESPONSIBLE STOP MONEY NO OBJECT. The operator apparently had some trouble with the name. They probably thought it was a code. The telegram was signed; SHOT HIT.

The other envelope was addressed to me in thick crayon pencil. There was a sheet torn from a notebook inside. It just said; Ring me tomorrow morning. Clark.

It didn't sound particularly urgent. I looked at the telegram form again. It had been phoned in at eleven-thirty p.m. the previous night. I put the two messages down on my bedside table. It was now around five and the sky was beginning to lose its shade of impenetrable black between the edges of the curtains. I undressed in the dark, dropping my clothes in a heap at the side of the bed. I was dead before I hit the sack.

* * *

Thunder was rumbling in the surrounding hills and the windscreen was silvered with the first drops of rain as I drove Clark up the driveway of The Palisades. The door was opened to us by Captain Rodriguez; his face looked pale and strange in the gloom. Clark led the way up to the big room on top. There was no-one else about the corridors. Rodriguez had left us at the foot of the stairs. Lightning was flickering on the horizon as we came out on to the big balcony and started the descent down to where the General was waiting.

Clark had decided to call what he described as an emergency session; the paper he carried had a screaming front page spread on the two killings, which the writers felt to be linked, and Clark figured that the Cubans might strike pretty soon now that the whole thing was out in the open. Macklehenny was already at The Palisades to augment the guard on the General; right now he was the only one in the big room apart from Diaz himself, looking frailer than ever in his wheel-chair.

As we got down on to the same level the first real crash of thunder sounded and lightning flaring in the sky behind flung a criss-cross pattern of window bars across the carpet. The General sat silhouetted against the window, watching the growing storm. Then the motor on the wheel-chair whirred and he angled himself into position alongside the great sideboard.

'A drink, gentlemen,' he said.

'All quiet,' Macklehenny whispered to Clark as he went by.

Clark grunted and followed me down to where the General was waiting. The three of us stood in a semi-circle facing the window while the General was mixing the drinks; whiskies for us and a daiquiri for himself. He propelled the chair over to his desk. Lightning flared again as he lifted his glass.

'To the confusion of our enemies,' he said.

'I'll drink to that,' I said.

General Diaz motioned us into chairs. We dragged them over into a horse-shoe facing him. The General sat with his back to the window drapes. We were gathered round him rather like a war-time military conference.

'I gather you are all familiar with the story, gentlemen,' he asked.

Clark cleared his throat. 'I put Mr Faraday in the picture, General,' he said.

'Good, good,' he answered. 'Then I shall confine myself to a listening role for the moment. Perhaps you would be kind enough to explain the suggested course of action, Sheriff.'

'Firstly, I'd like to speak about some fresh information which has just come to hand,' said Clark.

The General nodded. His strong hands were clasped together on the blanket. The quiver of arrows was still strapped to the side of his chair and the bow itself was

203

close to hand on the top of his desk.

'Like I mentioned on the phone, General, I checked at the Fitzgeorge opposite yesterday,' Clark said. 'Mr Faraday's theory about the Carmen Benson shooting is one hundred per cent correct, I'd say. One man was responsible for what could only have been an attempt on your life. The country club manageress gave me a good description. And he had a set of fishing rods with him, she says. That would have been the rifle and telescopic sight. The doc was right. It was a Mannlicher, the lab tests showed, and the description of the man tallies with that of Damascus.'

Clark turned to me and passed over some photographs. He tapped one of them with a horny thumb. 'That's the trigger specialist,' he said.

The print was blurred, probably from a police file, but it was a good enough likeness; it showed a sallow, narrow face of typical Spanish appearance. The eyes were hard, the lips thin and compressed; the thin mustache and the dark shadows under the eyes completing a picture of a man I shouldn't have looked for at a Y.M.C.A concert.

'Why Damascus?' I said.

The General laughed a harsh, tearing laugh as thunder rumbled again in the gloom of the big room.

'He used to live in Damascus, sir,' he said, 'and the name stuck. A hardened professional killer who should have been executed at the time of the coup.'

Clark passed me three other pictures; two were Cubanos, types one sees a million times without remembering anything special. Plump faces which would have had olive complexions in the flesh; bushy black hair in the old photographs, now probably turning grey; dark eyes; one clean-shaven, one with a black mustache. The latter was a face I felt I might know if I looked at it long enough.

'Hernando,' said Clark, tapping the last picture with his thumb. 'Probably the ice-pick man. He looks the type.'

I had to agree with him. A long, jagged scar ripped his cheek from the corner of the mouth to his right eye-socket. His thin hair was powdered with grey. I spread out the pictures of the four men who had come to kill General Diaz on the desk and studied them again. A pale flicker of lightning died in a bluish flare beyond the window panes. The General sat stiff and proud in his chair; not even his hands moved on the blanket. They were about the only part of him visible in the twilight. Once again I admired his guts.

It was a tough quartet. But even without the General's other guards it was four against four if they came; counting the General, of course. But then you had to count in the bowman. That was probably why he practised every day. I looked at the four faces. They would be sure to come all right. If not this week, then next.

'Hernando would be rather difficult to hide,' I told Clark, indicating the scar.

'He keeps out of sight until he's ready to make his play,' said Clark. 'Leastways, that was the drill in Cuba, according to the General.'

'Correct, sir,' said the General, raising his glass.

Macklehenny went over and stared moodily out of the window at the darkening tree-tops.

'I've been doing some homework,' said Clark casually. 'I got the finger-man.'

The words dropped into the sudden silence so that the next crash of thunder, miles nearer across the rolling hills, underlined the impact.

'Go on,' said General Diaz, leaning forward almost imperceptibly in the chair; he looked about as interested in the information as if Clark had said he preferred whisky sour to milk as a nightcap. Macklehenny came back and stood behind the General, between him and the window.

'I went up to L.A. and did some research,' said Clark. 'Things been happening around here seemed a mite too pat. I tried the police files, then the Public Library. It was time well spent. Do you remember a man called Myers, General?'

Diaz frowned and lifted his tall glass to his lips; the next flash of lightning made a gaunt mask of his face. There was no accompanying clap of thunder this time.

'From Cuba, you mean?' He shook his head. 'Should it convey anything?'

'Trouble is, Myers knew you, General,' said Clark. 'And he put the finger on you. And Mr Holgren.'

Clark swilled the whisky around in his glass and squinted at it like it was below proof.

'When he was a younger man he was in Cuba as a motor agent,' he went on. 'He had the Ford concession for Havana and half a dozen other contracts besides. Later, he had a hand in supplying motorized transport for the Cuban Army. That was where he met the Hernando brothers. They were kindred souls. Myers was as rotten as they come. He and the Cubanos were involved in every type of racket and fraud. When the lid blew off and you indicted the Hernandos and their chums, Myers went to ground. After the coup misfired he surfaced and got a bit too clever. He was in another big swindle over motor deals and was sentenced to five years.'

'He did two and was then released. Inside, he had maintained contact with

208

Hernando. In the meantime you had retired and gone to live in the States under an assumed name. Myers blew out of Cuba. He would have been deported in any case. He returned to the U.S. changed his name and started in the garage business once more. But I recognized his photograph in some old newspaper files and that put me on the right slant. His wife had left him while he was in Cuba but he had a son and that wasn't very hard to check.'

'You're not talking about Cheney?' I said.

There was another tremendous clap of thunder which made the whole house shake. Clark blinked in the white glare which followed.

'One and the same,' he said. 'Cheney kept in touch with his old pals over the years. And as luck would have it he took the Redbarn business in Mudville a while ago, only a few miles from where the General was living. The Cubanos had never given up and when he heard they were being released, he tipped them off.'

'Hoping to gain what?' I said.

Clark shrugged. 'Money, perhaps. In any event he's just a mean cuss. He realized the General wouldn't remember him from the old days. In the meantime he kept his eyes open and passed information along. I must admit Mr Holgren's death is largely guesswork, but it shouldn't be too difficult to check. Supposing he ran into Hernando, or the four Cubans together in L.A. He would have recognized them, of course, as he worked with you on the prosecution case in Havana, General. He realized you would be in deadly danger. He tries to reach you but you are away.'

'So he drives up, passing me on the way,' I said. 'When he gets to Mudville, Hernando had already warned Cheney by phone. Or perhaps Holgren by an unlucky coincidence stops at Cheney's place for gas. But however it came out, Hernando must have recognized Holgren in L.A. anyway, because he's not far behind. Cheney asks Holgren into his office on some pretext. When they go to the car Hernando is hiding on the back seat. Cheney pulls a gun on Holgren, forces him to drive around Mudville. Then Hernando makes his play and batters Holgren with the pick, I drive by and the two men hide in one of the gardens until I've gone to fetch the Sheriff.'

'Then they drive Holgren to the river for a midnight bathe,' said Macklehenny sourly. 'There was another car up there, that they came back in. We found more tracks on the road.'

There was a long silence. The General sat slumped in his blanket; only his yellow eyes seemed alive in the dark recesses of his face.

'Undoubtedly the correct sequence of events, gentlemen,' he said at last. 'I must congratulate you both. However, following the attempt with the rifle we may assume our friends have had a change of plan. It has now been more than two weeks since they made any positive move.'

'We can't be sure of that,' said Clark sharply. 'We don't know what they've been doing or what their movements were. You may have been in danger any one of a dozen ways without knowing it.'

The General sighed. His voice sounded very tired as he replied.

'Life can be a burdensome thing, gentlemen. I cannot say that I would be really sorry to see a term put to my existence.'

'You mustn't say that, sir,' said Macklehenny with rising heat.

The General stirred and passed his hands across the bow on the desk in front of him.

'You are, of course, right, Mr Macklehenny,' he said. 'Forgive me, gentlemen. I think I had better ring Valdar at the gate. We have much to discuss.'

He propelled the wheel-chair over towards the grey plastic telephone. He lifted the receiver and held it to his ear. I saw a puzzled expression on his face. He jiggled the receiver rest and then put it stiffly back.

'There is no reply from the gate,' he said in tones from which surprise had drained all emotion.

'Perhaps the storm put the line out,' said Clark, still not comprehending.

'Storm nothing,' I said, sliding out of

my chair as another crack of thunder sounded.

'Keep your eyes peeled, Clark. I got a feeling this is it.'

★  ★  ★

Clark and Macklehenny got up without hurry and covered the General without seeming to.

'I'll have a looksee at the front,' I told Clark. He patted his revolver butt. I took his point. I had the Smith-Wesson out as I went down the big staircase that led to the main hall. I passed Rodriguez in the corridor. He saluted and hurried on towards the General's room. I called after him but he didn't stop. Thunder was rumbling again as I got down by the main entrance. There was something definitely wrong.

When I pulled at the main door it wouldn't budge. Then I saw that it was locked and the inside key was missing. Fanning the gun I stepped over to the window flanking the porch. It was now almost dark outside and I couldn't see a thing. I found a panel of three brass switches alongside the front door; I flipped them on and off experimentally. Two controlled the hall and staircase lighting. The third lit the porch. I went cautiously back to the small window and peeked through.

One of the Dobermanns was lying not more than three yards away, at the edge of the porch. It was spread out unnaturally still; I watched it for nearly half a minute. It was either dead or doped. I switched off all the lights and stepped back into the hall. I saw the half-open door and a thin bar of light coming up. I pushed the door all the way open; rough steps led down into some sort of cellar.

Warm, oil-heated air came up to me. I took the safety-catch off the Smith-Wesson and put out a foot into the darkness; the brushing finger tips of my left hand found a switch on the wall. Neons blinked into trembling radiance. I went down the stairs into the boiler room. In one corner an oil furnace for the General's central heating rumbled to itself with controlled power. Light flickered on to the gritty floor through a yellow heatproof glass panel.

The cellar was a large, shadowy place and there were a lot of peculiar marks on the dust of the floor. On the far side was a coke heap. To the left of this was an enormous old solid fuel boiler that looked like something out of the engine room of the Titanic. It evidently hadn't been used since it was superseded by the oil-fired unit. But someone had been using it recently.

A piece of khaki-coloured cloth protruded from the edge of the rusted furnace door that was half the height of a man. I lifted up the heavy iron latch on the front of the furnace. Something sagged out at me, something that had once been human. It was clad in shirt and underclothes and had been thrust, half-kneeling in among the ashes. The shirt and front of the face were stained and clotted with blood and the eyes stared fixedly in front of them with that far-seeing look the dead always have, like they know what lies beyond the stars.

I had a job to keep the furnace door

steady as that face came at me out of the darkness. Belsen-like it swung against the side of the boiler and showed me the whitened bone of the brain pan. An object fell down tinkling into the ashes at my feet. Someone had been fooling with ice-picks for the second time in my experience.

# 12

## Electric Chair

I held the door with one hand and reached for an iron slicing bar with the other. I put the bar against the corpse's chest and levered him back into his iron coffin. Then I slammed the oven door and latched it. The triangle of shirt still stuck out. The oil furnace roared and bubbled to itself; it made a sinister sound in the depths of the cellar. The old familiar scratching was round the base of my spine and my forehead was wet and clammy. It didn't come from the heat of the furnace either. I stood and thought for ten long seconds. Nothing moved in the house above.

Then I took off my jacket, unbuckled my holster. I got out the revolver again and unscrewed the silencer. I put the silencer in the spring-clip holster, put some spare slugs on the cellar floor beside me, wrapped the harness round the holster and buried it among the coke. I wiped my hand clean on the handkerchief. Then I took the Smith-Wesson and shoved it down inside the sock on my right leg. The barrel fitted just inside my shoe without too much trouble. I was afraid it might fall out when I walked but I tried it a few times up and down the cellar and it worked.

Then I had a better idea and transferred it to my left instep so that I could get at it easier with my right hand. The Smith-Wesson held five slugs. I took the other five I'd put on the floor and made them into a small flat package, using an old envelope from my pocket. I shoved that down inside my right sock, just inside the shoe. When I tried walking again it wasn't too uncomfortable. I put my jacket on.

I transferred the slicing bar to my right hand and went upstairs again very fast but very light; we might have ten minutes at most. When I got to the balcony I saw Rodriguez standing along the end of the corridor; he looked worried. The shock didn't register until I got down to the ground floor and up to the General. Another great booming cannonade of thunder sounded like it was going to bring the roof in with it. The electric-blue glare of the lightning gave Rodriguez' face a deathly pallor; I could see his eyes twitching even underneath the dark side-blinders he wore.

'Who can you rely on here tonight?' I asked the General.

'Two at the gate, one man in the grounds,' said Diaz. 'The Captain there, we four. Gomez and one of the guards are away in L.A., I don't count the servants, of course.'

'We got company,' I told him.

I sketched in what had happened downstairs. Clark's lips tightened and he moved his hand towards the butt of his gun. I stopped him.

'Take it nice and easy,' I said. 'We're being watched.'

The General's yellow eyes were unblinking as ever; he didn't move a muscle as I explained the set-up.

'Thank you, Mr Faraday,' he said as I

finished. 'I think you can leave this to me.'

He called Clark and Macklehenny over to his chair and spoke with them in a low voice. Rodriguez looked down curiously from the stair-head. I went and sat in one of the General's chairs and smoked a cigarette. I wondered why he didn't put the main lights on.

The General called me over. 'I'm going up top,' he said. 'Please stay with Sheriff Clark and do as he says. Whatever you see happening, stay put. Is that clear?'

I nodded. Diaz smiled. Macklehenny came up behind the chair and pushed it towards the bottom of the left-hand staircase. Clark stood looking up the stair-head until he heard the whirr of the lift. Macklehenny walked up the stairs, keeping pace with the General's chair on its electrically operated platform. When they got to the top, the General said something to Rodriguez. The Captain saluted and went off down the corridor.

Clark came over to me in the gloom and gripped my arm; we went to the foot of the right-hand staircase and waited in the semi-darkness. I could hear a faint shuffling. I noticed that the Sheriff had the General's bow and the quiver of arrows. I didn't know what the hell was going on. We waited for perhaps a quarter of a minute. The only lights in the vast room came from a couple of shaded lamps down near the General's desk, which had been switched on at dusk. In the half of the window not masked by the curtain, the blue glare of the storm played a will-o-the-wisp dance macabre among the tree-tops and the hills beyond. Boris Karloff might have been at home here but I wasn't.

Then I heard the soft thump of Rodriguez' feet coming back down the top corridor. Almost at the same moment, from the dark stair-head behind us came the well-known whine and the squeaking of rubber-treaded tyres on the General's wheel-chair. As the lightning flickered again, Clark and I could see the chair silhouetted on the balcony; it passed the top of the staircase at an incredible speed and made off down the corridor. The note of the electric motor made a high, shrill scream that sounded even above the racket of the storm. The chair went on down the landing towards Rodriguez with increasing velocity.

I heard the Captain stop and shout in alarm. There was a shuffling on the staircase behind us but Clark and I had no time for it. The hollow boom of a shot sounded high above another rising peal of thunder. In the flare of the next lightning flash I saw the General's figure hunched oddly in his blankets; the chair went straight at the Captain as he emptied his revolver into the helpless form of the General. A bullet spanged off metal. As I leapt forward, Clark's hand was on my shoulder, forcing me down. Rodriguez kicked at the chair as it reached him; for a moment he and the chair tottered at the top of the left-hand staircase in the flash of the lightning.

Incredibly, I found the General at my elbow. He was wheezing and puffing after dragging himself painfully down the stairs behind us. He held the bow that Clark had passed him. The steel arc sang against the boom of the thunder and the great organ-notes of the string sounded

222

again. The steel bolt whistled in the air. Rodriguez screamed once and twisted as the shaft went through his throat, came out the other side.

He grasped the wheel-chair with dying hands and brought it crashing the length of the stairs with him. The motor shrieked as the wheels left the floor, and the big metal chair bounced and trembled its way down the flight, dragging the recumbent figure of the Captain with it. His twitching hand tightened on the rail of the chair and then was still. Thunder boomed again as Clark wiped his face. He went over and switched off the motor of the wheel-chair. The wheels ceased their frantic spinning.

'Well done, Howard Hill,' I told the General.

The whole room sprang into light as Macklehenny flung the switch. He walked down the stairs behind us. The General sagged back and I helped him into a chair. His face was white and chalky with the effort of dragging himself down the steps. Clark released the Captain's dead hand from the rail of the chair and righted the whole thing. He tossed out the bundled pillows and blankets with which Macklehenny had duplicated the figure of Diaz. He and the deputy righted the chair awkwardly. It seemed to work all right, except that one of the rails was bent. Clark and Macklehenny helped the General back into the chair. Clark went over to Rodriguez and lifted away the dark cheaters. 'Julio,' he grunted. Then I remembered the photographs he'd showed me earlier. The one with the moustache. It would have had to be him. He looked most like Rodriguez.

'The General figured he'd crack when the chair came at him,' he said softly, almost to himself. He rubbed his chin and looked across at me.

'He killed Rodriguez somewhere in town,' I said, 'and took his place. I thought he looked a bit strange tonight. That's why he stood a long way off whenever the General spoke to him. Drove back in the car past the gate men. He hid the Captain's body in the furnace room and poisoned or drugged the dogs. Rodriguez was in charge of feeding them.

Question is, were the others with him, or was he supposed to let them in?'

'My bet is that they're inside the house,' said Clark. 'We haven't heard a word from the servants. And the phone's cut off from the gate and the outside. The guards would have been up to investigate if they'd been able.'

The General nodded slowly. 'I'm afraid the Sheriff is right, gentlemen,' he said.

He sat looking down at the body of Julio. He prodded it curiously with the end of his bow; blood was coagulating where the steel tip of the shaft stuck out beyond the neck muscles. Remembering Rodriguez in the boiler room I couldn't feel sorry.

'Thank you, Mr Clark,' Diaz said to the Sheriff, 'for agreeing to my little plan. Melodramatic and unnecessary, of course, but for a minute there I felt my old self again.'

His eyes flashed and sparkled. Twenty years seemed to have dropped off his age. I went over to the table and lit another cigarette.

'That leaves three, then,' I said.

'And Myers,' Macklehenny reminded me.

'And Myers,' I agreed.

As I spoke dark figures came into focus on the balcony.

'I said we'd got company,' I told Diaz. 'Meet the Four Just Men.'

# 13

## Three from Cuba

The persuasive black snout of a Schmeisser machine pistol focused unwaveringly on our small group round Julio. The barrel looked as big as a mine-shaft and it seemed centred dead on my belly. It was very necessary not to move. I stayed so still it felt like my feet were nailed to the floor. Clark and Macklehenny had frozen too; in any case no-one could have done anything because of the General.

Only he seemed perfectly at ease; he sat back in the chair, fingering the string of his bow almost sensually and looked at the three men who stood on the balcony. I couldn't see Myers though I guessed he wouldn't be far away. The one with the machine pistol I took to be the man they called Damascus. That was why I hadn't moved.

The medium-sized man holding the

sub-machine gun, resting the squat black barrel gently on the staircase railing before him could only be Salivar. But it was the one with the automatic and looking nowhere in particular, though all his attention was evidently fixed on the General, who arrested my gaze. Hernando's picture hadn't done him justice. He stared about him for a moment or two longer, sizing up the situation. Then another shadow moved on the balcony and the big, thickset form of the man I had known as Cheney came forward into the light.

It was the General who finally broke the silence which had superseded the low growl of receding thunder.

'You have not changed, Hernando. Jackals always gather in packs.'

Hernando didn't say anything. He looked down at the body of Julio and smiled. I thought it was the most sinister thing I had ever seen. I wasn't anxious to see him in an unpleasant mood. He moved the automatic in a steady arc, stopping momentarily on each of us in turn.

'Weapons on the floor,' he said. 'Slow's the word.'

I put down the slicing bar as ostentatiously as possible. The General placed his bow on the floor by his chair. I saw Clark and Macklehenny exchange a brief glance. Then they unbuckled their gunbelts and dumped them on the carpet.

Hernando turned. 'Go down and search them, Myers,' he said. The big man raised a shaky hand in protest.

'Why didn't you call me Cheney?' he whined. 'That's what I'm known as here.'

'You don't think you're fooling these people any?' said the man called Damascus. 'They was wise to you a long while ago.'

His voice sounded like a rusty gate. Myers flushed and came on down the stairs towards us. He looked about as lethal as a flit-gun. If Damascus had said anything else to him I felt he might have bust out crying. He ran me over with his unsteady hands. A blast of whisky blew in my face.

'Stand to one side of him, you bloody

229

fool,' said Hernando without heat.

Myers obliged. As he went he caught me a blow across my right cheek with his flattened hand. I put my knuckles in his belly with enough force to make him wince with pain.

'Right, Cheney,' I said. 'That squares us off.'

'Quit the fooling,' said Damascus, 'or I'll let you have a slug together with these creeps.'

Myers went over me again; he searched as far as the knees but found nothing. The barrel of the Smith-Wesson was making a comfortable pain against my left foot. While he went through the motions with Clark and Macklehenny the three men came down the staircase and joined us on the floor; the storm was dying away now but the rain still battered at the windows and an occasional flicker of lightning showed beyond the tree-tops. The Cubans came down the stairs one at a time, covered by the others.

After Myers had finished, the one called Salivar put down the machine gun and searched us again; he didn't do any better at it than Myers. I was glad Damascus stayed put. He would have made a more efficient job of it than either of them.

'Sit down over there,' said Hernando. He pushed the General's wheel-chair to the other end of the room, near the desk. The others dragged over three of the big padded chairs. We all sat in line abreast watched by the trio. They didn't relax for a second.

Myers was still grumbling to himself.

'You'd better make this worth my while,' he said to Hernando.

'I'm finished in this town.'

'You'll be finished altogether if you don't button up,' Damscus told him, with a slight wave of the Schmeisser. 'You'll be taken care of, like we said.'

Myers went and sat down on a long divan and folded his hands over his stomach; his face looked patched and blotchy, like he'd been drinking all evening.

Clark spoke for the first time. 'This here's a private dick from L.A.,' he said, jerking his thumb at me. 'This ain't his case. We're the professionals.'

He smiled across at me, indicating Macklehenny's badge and his own in the same gesture of his thumb.

'It's his case now,' said Hernando. 'We need hostages for safe conduct. Just make sure your usefulness doesn't run out, that's all.'

He looked away to include Myers in his remark.

'Why Holgren?' I asked Hernando.

He turned to look at me properly. It was the only real direct look he gave me from first to last.

'What's this man's name?' he asked Myers. Myers told him.

'It can't make any difference now, Faraday,' Hernando said. 'He spotted us in L.A. We all met up on the street one afternoon. He recognised us. We checked up his business address and staked the place out. Myers had kept us in the picture and we'd known Holgren in Cuba. I knew he wouldn't be able to say a lot over the phone. I wanted our arrival to be a surprise for the General.' He smiled across at Diaz sitting upright in his chair.

The General said nothing, just looked at him with those emotionless eyes.

'We got on to Myers and I followed Holgren in my own car. Myers had instructions to stop him at the garage on any pretext. As it happened, he stopped of his own accord. Myers asked him into the office and I got in the back seat of the Bugatti.'

'Then you're the ice-pick expert?' I said.

Hernando smiled again.

'You guessed the rest,' he said. 'When we'd done the job you came along and stopped. You were lucky, Faraday. We had a gun on you from behind the hedge.'

'I didn't see any other car around,' I said.

Hernando made a clicking noise with his tongue. The scar on his cheek twitched as though with inward laughter.

'You're not dealing with amateurs. We left it at the garage. Myers went back on foot to get it while I drove Holgren out to the Agano. Then we came away together. It was a pity about the Bugatti. It was a nice heap.'

'Where were you hanging out the last few weeks?' said Clark.

'We have a big organisation,' said Hernando. 'And the answer to your question is restricted information. We stayed holed up in L.A. until we needed to come out here.'

'Who did the first-rate job on the Benson girl?' I said. 'Just to tie up the loose ends. She was my assignment.'

Hernando flicked the muzzle of his automatic towards Damascus.

'The expert,' he said. 'One of those coincidences we meet sometimes. Eh, hombre?'

Damascus twitched up his face in what I took to be a smile. His knuckles tightened on the grip of the machine pistol.

Hernando turned back to the General. 'But one's misfortune is another's gift, as we say back home, General.'

Another faint reverberation of thunder echoed through the room as the storm spent itself on the blunted spikes of the distant hills.

'What have you done with my

servants?' the General asked him levelly. His voice was steady but his eyes burned with a kind of pale fire.

'No need for alarm, senor,' Hernando told him. 'They are safely locked in their quarters. I told them all here would be shot if they make a disturbance. They knew we mean it. So . . . '

He shrugged. He turned to Clark and Macklehenny.

'You wonder how we get in, eh? Well, the information do you no good so I tell you. It is quite simple. Julio there was the most like Rodriguez, with whom we have an old score to settle. We choose a night when he come into town with the big station wagon. For three nights nothing happen. Then he comes in alone and stops for gas. Tonight.'

He paused as a brief flash of lightning spent itself against the dark window panes.

'We treat him the same as Holgren. Then Julio dress in his clothes and the dark glasses. The rest of us lie on the floor of the wagon while Myers comes behind with our surprise. The guards have no suspicion when we get to the gate. We get inside and overpower them. We let Myers in and cut the telephone wires. After we get inside the house Julio drugs the dogs while we round up the servants. Simple. Yet a perfect operation of its kind.'

He scratched the scar on his cheek with the muzzle of the automatic with ill-concealed pleasure. 'So you kill Julio. An eye for an eye . . . '

'You made a good job of it,' Clark told him. 'But you won't get away with it.'

Hernando showed his teeth once more. 'We shall see, senor. As I said we are a big organisation. We have made more than adequate plans. And this has been a meeting I shall treasure for years.'

'The Sheriff's right,' said the General. 'But as it is me you want and nobody else, why involve others? Shoot me and let them go.'

Hernando went over and looked down at him. The scar stood out in an angry red line on his cheek.

'General, you do not understand the situation,' he said. 'A few weeks ago that was exactly our intention. Now there has been a change of plan. Perhaps you have not seen the papers. No matter. There has been a coup. The Government has been overthrown and our own party is once again in power. I received a radio message three nights ago. You are wanted at home. To stand trial for treasonable activities, you understand. The verdict is inevitable, of course. Ironic is it not? Remembering that this is the exact reversal of the situation when you condemned my brother. We do not forget those years we rotted in gaol.'

The old man didn't make any reply but just sat looking steadily at him. Hernando was the first to glance away.

'You've got courage, senor, that I will say,' he said with reluctant admiration. 'But bullets deal with courage just as efficiently as with the cowardly.'

Once again he glanced over at Myers who had found one of the General's Scotch bottles and was shakily pouring himself a slug. Damascus' machine pistol hadn't deviated one inch from the four of us while Hernando had been talking. Salivar sat on a chair and balanced the tommy gun on his knee. He looked like he knew how to use it.

'So you see why we need these men, General,' said Hernando. 'As sureties for your good conduct.'

He glanced round the room.

'So you might as well make yourselves comfortable. Drinks all round.'

Myers got up and went to the General's big cocktail cabinet and started setting up Scotch glasses; he didn't ask anyone what they wanted.

Hernando waved his automatic expansively. 'Providing no-one gets any stupid ideas it shouldn't be too intolerable a wait.'

He passed round the glasses Myers handed him. We all drank. The Scotch tasted good. I felt the gun barrel secure against my leg and the packet of cartridges in my other sock. There was only one thing to do and that was to hang on. I settled back in the chair and loosened my tie.

'Get what rest you can,' said Hernando. 'We leave at dawn.'

★ ★ ★

It was around five when I woke up again. The storm had died away and my mouth tasted like a rat's nest. Salivar slept quietly in a chair with his mouth hanging slack. The General was still sitting bolt upright, deep in thought. His untasted whisky glass sat on the tray clipped to the side of his chair; his unseeing yellow eyes faced Hernando. The latter sat with the automatic in one hand and his glass in the other and as much at ease as I'd ever seen him.

Damascus was standing up, with his back supported against a table; the Schmeisser raked the room from time to time. He looked tireless and indestructible. I figured he was the most deadly of the three, despite Hernando's virtuosity with ice-picks. If we could eliminate him we had a chance. Macklehenny was sleeping. Clark sat and smoked. His face told me nothing. Myers was lying on a divan snoring heavily. His empty whisky glass had rolled under a table. From time to time Damascus looked at him in disgust.

'Time to be moving soon,' said Hernando to no-one in particular: I blinked and sat up. The Schmeisser stopped its traverse and steadied on my gut.

'I suppose it's no good telling you guys to give up this crazy idea?' said Clark. Hernando shook his head.

Clark sighed. 'I guessed not,' he said. 'But you'll never make it out of here. You figure to get the General back to Cuba? You must have a few marbles missing.'

Hernando didn't even blink. 'I don't know why I'm telling you,' he said, 'but I am. We got three hostages, apart from the General, right? No-one knows we're here.'

'What about the cut telephone?' said Clark. 'There could be a posse outside right now.'

Damascus smiled. Hernando shook his head again. 'We repaired the phone last night. If anyone had rung the General couldn't be disturbed. Don't delude yourselves, gentlemen.'

'And the guards at the gate?' Clark

said. 'They've had all night to break loose.'

'We know our business,' Hernando said. 'Shackled with their own handcuffs to a solid iron stove down in the cellar. Gagged. And with their feet bound as well. Let's be realistic.'

'But you really think you can take a conspicuous character like the General out of this district without being spotted?' I said. 'Last night, yes, but it'll soon be daylight. So you get him out of the county. But out of the country's another thing altogether.'

Hernando smiled like he was dealing with children.

'You're talking about a government,' he said. 'Dealing with an enemy of the state. So we got a government's resources. The little surprise downstairs will take care of the General and his wheelchair. About ten miles down the road a ways there'll be a helicopter. It's big enough for all of us. Any questions?'

He might have been lecturing on political economy. He looked round the room. There were no questions. Macklehenny had woken up. Everyone's faces looked grey in this early morning atmosphere. There was no sign of dawn; wouldn't be for hours yet but it had that unmistakeable feel of early morning. That and the taste in my mouth. Unless we could come up with something we were finished. I knew one thing. Hernando and his chums weren't taking any of us on any helicopter except the General. We had perhaps an hour at the house and possibly half an hour on the journey to the rendezvous with the chopper.

I decided to wait until the journey; that would provide what chances there might be. It was either that or die here. And none of the three men guarding us so closely were likely to care which way we went out. My one worry was that the General might be rash enough to make an unguarded move.

'Waken that sot,' said Hernando, pointing to Myers. Damascus got up and prodded the big man with the muzzle of the machine pistol. He woke up snuffling and cursing.

'Cut it out,' he said thickly to Damascus.

'On your feet and make yourself useful,' said Hernando. Myers got up quickly. He rubbed his hands across his blurry eyes once or twice.

'What time is it?' he said.

'Time you started pulling your weight in this outfit,' said Damascus prodding him again with the pistol.

'Lay off,' snarled Myers. 'I haven't had my cut yet.'

'You'll get yours,' Damascus promised him. Anyone less dumb and stupid than the big garage owner might have read more significance into the remark but he only grunted, ferreted for the whisky glass and poured himself another shot.

'And cut out that stuff,' Hernando told him. 'We might need you later.'

Damascus stepped forward and knocked the glass out of Myers' hand with a swift movement of the pistol barrel; the glass broke as it hit the floor and the whisky soaked into the carpet. Myers' eyes glinted redly and his fists balled at his side.

243

'Try something,' Damascus invited him softly.

Myers stood irresolute and then relaxed his hands and turned away. The whirring of the motor on the General's wheel-chair was like an electric shock in the quiet room. The muzzles of the three Cubans' weapons converged on the General like the well-oiled movements of a battle ship's turret guns and a dozen times as quickly. The General turned his chair and came slowly towards us.

'It seems to me, gentlemen,' he said, 'that it is likely to be a strenuous day. Have you any objection to breakfast?'

'We haven't got time for all that,' said Damascus sullenly.

'It won't take long,' said the General blandly. 'If one of you will tell my housekeeper Inez to prepare something she will know what to do. Tell her my usual breakfast and not to forget the ketchup.'

'This sounds like a trick . . . ' burst in the man called Salivar.

'Don't be ridiculous,' said the General evenly. 'Myers can go and give the instructions. That is, if all my domestic staff haven't been murdered by your gang of gaol-birds.'

'Bring the woman up here, Myers,' said Hernando. It was the first time I had heard irritation in his voice. 'And go with him, Salivar. Make sure nothing goes wrong.'

He tossed a bunch of keys at the Cuban. The two men went out up the stairs. Macklehenny and Clark and I stretched and looked at one another. I sneaked a glance at my watch. It was already half-past five. I still couldn't think of anything that gave us half a chance. Only the General seemed unperturbed. I thought there was even satisfaction in his heavy eye-cavities as he looked proudly in front of him. Myers and Salivar came back with a thin-faced, pale woman with short black hair tending to grey; she looked like she hadn't slept all night.

'Don't be worried, Inez,' the General told her kindly. 'Everything is in order. I should like my usual breakfast. You can bring me a tray. Sandwiches for the rest.

245

And two flasks of coffee.'

'We haven't got time for all this,' Damascus broke in impatiently 'We leave at six.'

'We can eat as we go,' said the General softly. The housekeeper hovered anxiously; her dark eyes fixed on those of the General. He gave her a gentle smile. The housekeeper looked at Hernando inquiringly. He nodded slowly.

'And hurry,' he barked. He motioned to Salivar to go with her. When they had gone out the two Cubans sat down again and carefully lined up their guns on the four of us spread out in front of them. I measured the distance but it just wasn't worth it. The odds were too great. And the General would get it first, which would defeat the object of the exercise.

Presently Salivar came up to the big room to say that the food was ready. The housekeeper had left everything in the hall. He had locked the staff in their quarters again. By now it was nearer half-past six. I wondered why Hernando had allowed the schedule to be fouled up.

Then I did a little simple arithmetic. It got light around eight. If we left right away we would be at the landing area soon after seven, if it was about ten miles like Hernando had said. That left an hour between our arrival and dawn. The Cubans would light flares or give some signal so that the helicopter could take them and the General off before first light.

'What about the dogs?' Damascus was asking Salivar.

'Still out,' he said. 'This twenty-four hour dope is really strong.'

Hernando got up. 'Let's move,' he said. Salivar guarded the General. He and Myers got Diaz on to the lift and started it up the left-hand staircase. The General looked around him like he didn't expect to see The Palisades again. I didn't feel much like betting on it either.

Hernando and Damascus kept the guns turned on Clark and Macklehenny and me. Then we went first up the right-hand staircase to meet the other party at the top. We all went down the big stairs to the main hall. Behind me I could hear Myers still whining something about his cut. Salivar and Damascus first carried the General's chair down the stairs between them, grunting at the weight. Salivar stayed in the hall to guard the General. Myers had the machine pistol now and he and Hernando stood behind us at the top of the stairs. Damascus came back up again and took the Schmeisser off Myers. We started the slow procession down the stairs. I was looking around for some way out when I heard Myers start up again.

'I've done more'n my share,' he was complaining to Hernando, 'so why shouldn't I get my cut now? How do I know you'll keep your word when we get to Cuba?'

'Shut your mouth,' said Damascus. 'You'll get your cut when it's time and not before.'

'This is as far as I go,' Myers blustered. 'If I blew what I knew you'll all be back up the river.'

I had a funny instinct about the way things were shaping. Hernando stood at the top with the pistol. Clark and

Macklehenny were to my front and at the side of the wall. The General and Salivar were out of the way down in the hall. That left me in the middle of the staircase with Myers right behind me and the trigger-happy Damascus with the Schmeisser right behind him. I didn't like that very much.

Something cold was breathing on my neck and there was an itching right between my shoulder blades. The warm bite of the Smith-Wesson chafed my instep, as I trod lightly and edged over to get between Clark and Macklehenny at the staircase edge. I had got over about two feet when shouting started behind me. The Schmeisser suddenly blammed twice, the two shots blurring together they were so close. Something like a warm wind went past my left cheek; there was a choking noise and the body of Myers passed me. He buckled at the waist like a toy doll, the breath whistling in his throat. Big scorch marks spread across the back of his blue suit and little white and blue flames rimmed the holes the bullets had made.

The burning lapped the dark stains and became smoke. Myers retched once or twice, clawed the air and then went down the whole length of the stairs. His body left scarlet splashes on the treads. It bounced once or twice when it got to the hall and brought a small table and some flowers down with it. Myers was dead by the time he got there, I figured. There was a clicking behind me and the empty cartridge cases scampered down the heavy pile stair-carpet. Damascus blew into the breech of the machine pistol.

'I told him he'd get his share,' he said.

I stood with one foot farther down the staircase, the other higher up, my leg bent at the knee. I hoped my left leg wouldn't tremble.

There was a long silence, then Hernando said, 'Nice and slow, gentlemen, and no tricks.'

We went down the staircase, stepping over the body of Myers. Salivar used the rest of the water in the upset vase to douse the smouldering cloth on Myers' back.

'Sorry about the mess, General,' he said pleasantly.

There came a muffled hammering on the kitchen door. It stopped when Damascus screamed at the staff to shut up. He had a glinter in his eye which I didn't like. I decided I would try to drop him first, whatever happened.

Salivar wheeled the General out into the hall and unlocked the main door. Hernando ordered us to pick up the food and walk in front of them. I picked up the General's big tray, which was covered by a white cloth; Clark and Macklehenny followed me with packages of sandwiches and the flasks of coffee. It was a hell of a time for a picnic. Hernando and Damascus brought up the rear. They switched off the main lights, leaving only the porch.

It was a raw, cold morning, with more than a hint of fog. The Dobermann still sprawled rigidly outside the main door. The light shone across the strip of drive and showed the station wagon in which Salivar had brought back Rodriguez earlier that night. The porch light also

251

shone on the sleek sides of a white-painted ambulance which bore the stencil of the County Ambulance Service.

'The surprise I spoke about,' said Hernando. 'We shouldn't have much trouble in getting through with this.'

# 14

## Death of a General

Salivar opened up the back of the ambulance and switched on the light inside. Hernando stood by with the Schmeisser as Clark and Macklehenny lifted the General's chair up into the ambulance; I couldn't see his face. Salivar had got inside and pulled the chair into the centre. There were four big metal strips screwed into the middle of the floor.

The General's chair just went between them; Salivar rummaged about in a locker and came up with four lengths of steel cable attached to spring clips. He clipped the cables from the arms and back rest of the General's chair down to the struts on the floor. The whole thing was now securely fastened to the body of the ambulance.

I stood at the rear of the vehicle; the

cold was biting and I hadn't got my trench coat. Though we had only one gun between the four of us and that difficult to get at, the odds were now in our favour if it came to a showdown. The thought had evidently occurred to the Cubans for Hernando and Damascus stood right behind us with the machine pistol and the sub-machine gun which Hernando had taken from Salivar. They watched with some impatience while the General was stowed into the big machine.

I handed up the General's tray to the Cuban and he passed it over on to the front of Diaz' wheel-chair. Then I saw him lean over and tear out the wire from the controls of the electric motor at the back of the chair. If we could unclip the chair and use the motor it would have made a useful weapon to ram the General out through the rear doors if it came to the pinch. Now that was out. Clark and Macklehenny got up in back with the General and laid out the sandwiches and coffee on top of a big locker that ran along the side.

Salivar went round to the driving seat

of the ambulance and started her up. He had to give four pulls of the starter; the motor was cold and damp in this foggy atmosphere. Then she coughed and broke into a roar. Salivar kept the choke out and then let her idle quietly. The exhaust smoke came up heavy and acrid in our nostrils. Hernando went back into the porch and doused the main house light. I could hear faint knocking now from the staff quarters.

'Phone wires cut again?' Hernando asked Damascus. He inclined his head.

'Up in the back,' he said, pushing the machine pistol into my side. I climbed up with Clark and Macklehenny. Salivar had gotten a long white coat on now, like a hospital intern My hopes of being able to make a break before dawn were beginning to ebb. Damascus kept the light on inside the ambulance when we started. We couldn't sit on the bunks either side because we could have been seen through the glass doors; for some reason they weren't frosted or painted black. This wasn't the genuine thing; even so, it would pass muster with nine out of ten people.

Hernando went over to the station wagon parked behind the ambulance. He came back and threw the ignition key into the bushes. Damascus climbed in with us and Hernando slammed the rear doors. Damascus sat down on a low level locker opposite us and nursed the pistol.

He put his free hand in front of him and motioned us down. We sat on the floor. Macklehenny was up against the bunk behind Salivar, who was driving; there was just a low wood partition between us and the driver and passenger seats. Nothing that would be of any use in stopping bullets. The General was slightly to the front of us, almost between Salivar and Hernando who had got into the passenger seat. He sat facing the rear and the muzzle of the tommy gun was all set to spray the interior.

Clark sat next to Macklehenny, and I sat in the middle of the ambulance floor and propped myself against the back of the General's chair. Damascus had myself and Clark clearly in view; Hernando covered Macklehenny and the General. It was as good an arrangement as could be devised, short of having us all lying on our faces on the floor. But if the ambulance was stopped for any reason it would be difficult to explain away. Not that the ambulance would stop. Hernando would simply blast his way out. Hernando turned round and smiled slowly at us. He also had put on a white coat.

'All set in back?' he said.

Damascus slapped the side of the partition with his clenched fist in reply. There was a pleasant aroma of liver and bacon. General Diaz had opened up the silver dish cover on his tray. He rubbed his hands. I looked over his shoulder and saw a ketchup bottle, silver salt cellar; the works. This was no wagon-lits but even so his breakfast looked pretty good. Except that I wondered how he could eat it when he was leaving behind a house containing three corpses and a room full of frightened domestics; he was made of strong material.

'Let's move,' said Hernando. The

engine throbbed, Salivar put her in first and we moved smoothly down the drive.

★ ★ ★

Branches tapped against the body of the big machine as Salivar took her round the curves in the drive; he drove well, keeping in low gear and not using the brakes at the corners. We ghosted down at about fifteen miles an hour; it was fairly steady inside here over the well-sprung chassis and the General's knife and fork started a steady rhythm that didn't cease until he'd finished his breakfast.

Mist swirled by the windows and Salivar had got his wipers going. We stopped at the gate and Salivar got out. He left the engine idling. All through he had made a minimum of noise; there wasn't much likelihood of waking up anyone who shouldn't have been awake. I glanced round. Damascus' Schmeisser came up imperceptibly at my gentle movement. Hernando had the tommy gun ready. I saw that the safetys on both weapons were off.

There came the clink of iron on iron as Salivar opened the gates. He drove gently through, past the mist-shrouded lodge. He drew up on the road and went back and re-locked the gate. I saw him throw the key away before he got back in the driving seat. Nothing moved in all the world. Salivar engaged the gear again and we pulled slowly away, moving northwards. I felt the perspiration gathering on my forehead; it was close in here, even though the night air was cold outside. Hernando had kept all the windows shut. The General's knife and fork kept up their measured click as the ambulance nosed along the quiet lane.

'Will you not join me, gentlemen?' said the General to everyone at large. 'The food is excellent.'

'We'll get clear of the area first,' said Damascus sourly. I could have done with a cigarette. It was becoming clear to me that I should have to think carefully before starting to get to the Smith-Wesson; it would have to look natural. If they handed out the sandwiches I might get an opportunity then.

I shot another glance over my shoulder. Macklehenny's face looked pale but he still had the crust to return me a wry wink; Clark had picked his people well. I knew he could be depended on if we got half a break. I felt certain I could take Damascus at the right moment, but that still left Hernando and the tommy gun, with the General right in the line of fire. Big odds but we had next to no choice. Once at the helicopter our limited usefulness as hostages was finished. It was a real mess, as they come; and they didn't come any better than this.

Salivar wasn't driving at more than twenty miles an hour; he kept to side lanes and evidently knew the way by heart. We met no other cars. The mist seemed to get thicker and then we started to go uphill. I caught a glimpse of my watch and saw that we had already been travelling about twenty minutes.

'How about that food, then?' said Clark. Damascus stood up and held the pistol at the ready.

'Don't try anything,' he said. Clark and Macklehenny started handing out the packets of sandwiches. Hernando shook his head. Damascus tore open a packet and started eating a sandwich, holding it in one hand. He still had his finger round the trigger.

The sandwiches weren't bad; my package contained a mixture of ham, cheese and sweet pickle. Any other time I might have been more critical but right now I was surprisingly hungry. Clark got out a flask of coffee; he poured the General's first. The housekeeper had provided plastic cups. It was scalding hot. It gave me an idea too; I hoped Clark would cotton on when the time came.

In ten minutes or so we would surely be getting near the area chosen for landing. It was already turned seven but Salivar showed no sign of faltering either in his speed or his sense of direction. I guessed the route had been driven over and timed not once but many times. There remained the supposition that the Cubans hadn't revealed their correct plan to us; that didn't matter a lot either and after daylight would be academic to most of us travelling in the back.

The darkness was growing imperceptibly lighter and I thought this was about the time. Within the next few minutes we would have arrived and once we were out of the ambulance it would be too late. I asked Clark to pass me another sandwich. I had to take it over my shoulder and I contrived to drop it on the floor.

I scrabbled around for it, smearing the sticky mixture of pickles and cheese on to my trouser leg. Damascus started snickering.

Under cover of mopping up the mess I had retrieved the Smith-Wesson and transferred it to my right hand. I got out a handkerchief and dabbed at the sandwich with my left hand while I leaned back on my right, holding the revolver behind me. I pushed off the safety catch with my thumb. Damascus thought I was merely supporting myself.

I put the handkerchief back into my pocket and glanced over my shoulder, asking Clark for another sandwich. I saw that both he and Macklehenny had seen the revolver. Clark had the half-full flask of boiling coffee in his right hand. It had the plastic top off. I hoped he knew what to do with it. He nodded slightly like he was replying to my question about the sandwich. I saw Macklehenny scramble into a different position against the bunk.

I turned back to Damascus leaving the revolver behind me. I got out the handkerchief again and put it over my legs. I offered a sandwich to Damascus but he waved it away. While I had the packet under his face I had picked up the revolver again with my right and put it under the handkerchief. It was going to be a difficult shot. I kept my hand there, pretending to hold the handkerchief in position. The barrel of the Smith-Wesson was pointed towards the ceiling of the ambulance and I should have to allow for the angle by bringing the barrel forward at the last minute.

I glanced at Hernando but his attention was taken up by Clark and Macklehenny. The General had finished his breakfast, and was drinking the coffee. Now seemed as good a time as any. I waited until Salivar changed gear at the top of a hill. Damascus, though still concentrating, was finishing off his sandwich. He had the Schmeisser barrel lowered an inch or two from the horizontal. I braced myself against the back of the General's chair and prayed for accuracy. I fired twice, shifting the barrel over a little each time. It was one of the most tricky pieces of shooting I'd ever attempted. The gun jumped and the roar and flare of the explosions momentarily deafened me. Powder smoke stung my cheeks and my trousers burst into flame where the slugs had passed through them, just over the top of the barrel.

The first shot missed and blew a hole in the top of the ambulance. But the second didn't. Though the angle was very shallow it seemed to go in Damascus' mouth and come out just over his eye. His body sagged and the Schmeisser fell on to the floor of the ambulance, where I kicked it over towards Clark. A fine spray of blood misted the bunks and particles of white substance flew about the interior of the ambulance. They appeared to be some of Damascus' teeth; not that he would be needing them any more. My ears were singing from the explosions.

As soon as the first shot sounded I heard Hernando scream. Clark had thrown the flask of scalding coffee in his face. He clutched at the back of the partition and the tommy gun fell on to the floor of the driving cab. Macklehenny was already up and had his braced arm round Salivar's neck. The ambulance swerved alarmingly and started to go off the road.

'Hold on, General,' I yelled. I was rolling towards the rear doors. I had my hand on the latch when the ambulance started to lurch, then it was turning over. Clark was slung along the interior after me and Damascus' body followed. We landed up in a heap of arms and legs against the rear doors. I could hear Clark scratching for the Schmeisser. He had the presence of mind to turn off the light in the back.

I had just got the door open when there was a tremendous crash and we were right off the road; I fell out and landed in wet bushes. I held tight to the Smith-Wesson and fell down an embankment. I heard Clark come after me. He yelled something to Macklehenny, then the sky was wheeling above me; it span faster and faster until I was hurled off the rim of the world.

* ★ ★ ★

I tasted blood and felt myself to see if anything was broken. I heard Clark groan and saw him get up from the wet earth a couple of yards away. I had been out only a few seconds but the sky was already lighter. I could see the ambulance heeled over, silhouetted against the sky at the top of the bank. It had gone off the road and rammed a tree before it could come down the scree-strewn slope. I recognised the roaring in my ears as an unnatural silence. I hoped the General was all right.

Then I heard two shots close together; they came from the interior of the ambulance. Clark and I had the same idea. Macklehenny hadn't got out. It could have been the deputy or the General. Or both. Unless Macklehenny had got to one of the guns. Hernando hadn't looked in too good a shape when we were thrown out. Then I heard the General's voice, precise, cool and controlled through the early dawn.

'Admirably done, Mr Faraday. An excellent piece of work.'

Clark smiled grimly. He got up wincing and I saw that blood was streaming from a rent in his pants.

'Just a graze on a rock,' he said. He lay down again and we started crawling towards the ambulance. Just then we both heard the faint sound coming from the north. It was the distinctive beat of a helicopter. I pulled Clark down. I had just seen someone get out of the ambulance. He dropped on the far side. I used the lull to get the package from my right shoe and re-load the Smith-Wesson. I now had a full chamber of five, with three in reserve. I didn't know how many the Schmeisser held but I felt we were a match for the Cubans. Would they try to break the General out or finish him off before they left? It was a calculated risk and the longer we left it the greater the danger.

Orange flame bisected the dark sky, throwing the area into harsh relief. The flare burnt brilliantly about a hundred feet from the ground and I could hear the rotor-blades of the helicopter change note, as the pilot thrashed the air on a different course, heading towards the signal. As the flare died, Clark and I wriggled farther along the bank. There was a fairly level area up ahead, which was evidently the rendezvous. If we could get there ahead of the Cubans we should have a better chance to intercept.

Just before the flare went into the ground, I saw two figures near the ambulance. There was no sign of Macklehenny and it was safer to assume that Salivar had survived the crash. The tommy gun hammered with heart-stopping suddenness and a chain of sparks burst the darkness in front of us as the bullets ricochetted from the stony ground. We went down the bank in a long, tumbling glide and found ourselves in a small plantation of trees. The tree boles weren't very thick but wide enough for our purposes.

Right now a sapling sixteen millimetres wide would have seemed enough after being out in the open. A tommy gun operating on exposed ground makes a man seem a mile high and at least forty feet wide. Clark was panting. I figured he was hurt worse than he had told me. He wasn't short on guts, that was for sure.

'How in hell do you work this thing?' he gasped.

I showed him. The Schmeisser's barrel was clogged with earth and it looked like it had struck a rock when Clark fell out of the back of the ambulance. I cleared the barrel. The tommy gun fired again while I was doing this. The bullets stitched across the edge of the thicket and went whining into the trees. One of the saplings near to us caught fire momentarily and then smouldered into darkness. The noise of the helicopter was nearer now. All the while we were stuck down here they could move the General to the machine without us being able to interfere.

'Keep the tommy gunner busy,' I told Clark. 'I'll try and work my way round behind.'

I had only gone a few yards off to the left, still within the cover of the thicket, when the Schmeisser barked. Clark only got off two or three shots. Then I heard his angry whisper through the trees. I crawled back towards him.

'The damned thing's jammed,' he said in exasperation.

'Try the single shot setting,' I said. I couldn't remember how many a machine pistol clip held but every burst was wasteful and we had to make each shot count. Clark fiddled about with the pistol. Then he sighted up towards a shadowy figure near the tree on the top of the bank. The pistol coughed once and I saw the tommy gunner duck back behind the tree.

'Get going,' said Clark with satisfaction.

I worked back through the small wood and a long way over to the left. It was growing too light for comfort and the helicopter still seemed to be searching around a little to the north. Twice more I heard Clark's gun and once a burst of tommy gun fire. By this time I was well over and the plantation and a shoulder of ground masked all my movements. I crawled cautiously up the rising slope and found myself back on the road again.

Keeping into the trees and tall grass which skirted the narrow highway, I gum-shoed quietly back towards the ambulance. I kept it between me and the gunner behind the tree. There was no sign of Hernando. I hoped he had gone on to signal to the helicopter but I couldn't bank on it. I got down on my knees and looked along towards the ambulance. It was about a hundred yards away now. Someone, probably Salivar, had closed the rear doors so I couldn't see inside. The General was keeping quiet.

So far as I could make out there was no-one hiding behind the big vehicle. Then the tommy gun hammered again and lances of flame licked out down towards the small wood where Clark was hiding. Bullets hummed like angry bees and made bright sparks on the stones. While the gunner was busy with his burst I ran in a fierce pulse of energy, keeping the ambulance between me and the tree. I looked around and then saw another flare lob up from the field several hundred yards ahead. That took care of one of the men. I couldn't have fixed a better time. I worked my way round the ambulance.

Clark wasn't firing now. I slowly raised my head over the edge of the driving cab window; I could only see the upper part of the tree. I held the Smith-Wesson in my right hand, safety catch off. With my left hand touching the tips of the grass I eased quietly round the front end of the ambulance. The gunner was down below me, with the tree between. I couldn't get a shot from here because of the lie of the ground and the way the branches spread but I could see enough to identify Salivar. Then the roar of the helicopter sounded louder; it swept over the tree-tops about a quarter of a mile away, looking like a gigantic mosquito looming out of the mist, its red and white navigation lights glowing like an insect's eyes.

Salivar turned his head to watch it. I chose that moment to jump. I hit a low branch of the tree with my head and deflected. I felt a blinding pain in my left arm as I hit the ground and then I landed on top of Salivar's legs. He went stiff with surprise and fear and we both slid forward down the bank. In the excitement I tried to hit him over the head with the Smith-Wesson. I missed but the barrel caught his knuckles a glancing blow and the sub-machine gun went bouncing down the bank before us.

By this time he had my gun hand and I was groping for his throat with my left; we went down through a bed of bracken and the flare hanging in the sky above us expanded until it filled the whole universe as I caught my head on a stone. My grip on Salivar's throat relaxed as we came to a halt in the scree. He got up with a sobbing cry. His boot, heavy with nails, stamped on my wrist and forced it into the mud. The Smith-Wesson fell from my fingers. Salivar went over and picked up the tommy gun while I fought for consciousness. He was quite deliberate about it. He came and stood over me and the smile on his face spread until it filled all my world.

The double crack of the explosion

seemed to rip through my body. The smile faded from Salivar's face. A long necklace of dark blood descended from his mouth towards the ground. He clutched at the spreading stains on his chest as his knees buckled. The tommy gun and his body hit the scree at the same time. I struggled up as Clark scrabbled into view nursing the Schmeisser.

'Thanks,' I panted. Clark looked white. The blood was pumping from his leg. He had to sit down. I went over and stuffed my handkerchief over his thigh. He got out his own handkerchief and bound that round it. It seemed to stop the bleeding.

'Take it easy,' I said. He nodded. I found the Smith-Wesson and cleaned the mud off it against my trousers. I went off along the bottom of the slope to where the light of the second flare was burning out in the smoky dawn. The air seemed split with engine noises. The big helicopter was down. It looked like an Army job; I should have estimated it would have held about ten or fifteen men. It was crudely camouflaged in the regulation brown and dark green affected by the military the world over.

It had no numbering or identification marks on it but then I wouldn't have expected it to have. The great rotor blades chopped at the dawn sky and the grass for yards around was blown flat by the rush of air. Hernando was half-leaning into the cabin talking to the pilot. In the stronger light which was creeping into the east he saw me coming. He loosed a shot with his automatic but it went wide.

Then he spoke to the pilot and the helicopter went straight up into the air and hovered, several hundred feet from the ground. Hernando set off running along the top of the bank. I cursed. I knew what he was going to do and I could have guarded against it. I hoped Clark would see him coming and get in a shot. I started uphill in the general direction of the ambulance, hoping that I could head Hernando off. It was a pretty forlorn hope what with the terrain I had to cover and my groggy condition. But at least I knew the General was alive or

Hernando would have lit straight out with the helicopter.

He must have known Salivar was finished. The chopper didn't make any attempt to follow us but simply hovered above the level ground; there was a steep shelf of rock farther on which descended into a ravine and the bank and belts of trees at this end made the spot where it hovered about the only practical landing point for some while.

I slipped and tore my way through the scree and the soaked grass. I could see Hernando now, bent double as he crossed the skyline obliquely in front of me. I risked a shot but it only sent stones scuttering a good two or three yards behind him. When I got on the level with bursting lungs Hernando was going like hell only a short way from the ambulance. There was no sign of Clark. I got up close to the big vehicle as I heard Hernando bang against the back doors. I went round the end at a reckless speed and made a right-angle turn.

Hernando was leaning half-in, half-out of the rear doors. I grabbed his leg and

276

pulled him off balance. He clung on to the door-handle as he came out with it. I fell to the ground as Hernando's gun crashed, filling the interior of the ambulance with smoke. A bitter sense of failure mingled with a sort of fury as I twisted Hernando's leg and smashed it against the metal steps at the rear of the ambulance. He gave a high scream and then the hand holding the automatic caught me across the throat and made me let go. The gun tinkled against the steps as it went down.

Hernando hesitated; the scar on his face twitched as he glared at me and then Clark came hobbling into view. He couldn't shoot because the Cuban was standing so close to me and the bullet would have gone into the interior of the ambulance. He did the next best thing and fired wide. Hernando shouted something in Spanish and set off running with jerky steps back towards the landing field. I got up, found the Smith-Wesson and pounded in pursuit. I saw Clark start limping after us.

The Cuban was still going well, despite

the roughing I'd given his leg. Long before I came up I saw that the helicopter was down, its rotor blades ticking over, as it waited for Hernando. It was quite light now and thin wisps of mist came up from the soaked ground and the long grass. I fired once at Hernando but my aim was erratic and he didn't slacken his stride, though he doubled about to put me off. Clark was a long way behind. I only hoped the heli pilot wasn't armed. The Cubano was my one ambition now that the General had gone.

I had three shots left and there was no time to re-load. The motor of the helicopter revved higher as Hernando drew near; the pilot lifted her and hovered about six feet above the ground. He meant to make as much height as he could straight away. I figured he would make as difficult a target as possible instead of giving us a side-on shot if he travelled backwards or forwards. I increased my pace. I was still more than a dozen yards away when Hernando jumped for it. He'd stuffed the automatic in his pocket and he caught the edge of the open door with both hands. The big machine was already lifting clumsily as he half-pulled himself inside.

Clark was closer now. I covered the last few yards. The helicopter was gathering speed and lifting but still no more than thirty feet above me. Hernando's feet were disappearing through the door. I chanced a shot, aiming for the tank. Every second decreased the chances. I squeezed the trigger, the Smith-Wesson coughed; metal spanged on metal with an angry scream I could hear even above the chopping of the blades. The perspex on the pilot's cabin blister starred. Clark dropped to his knees and started pumping deliberate single shots into the belly of the machine.

I sighted with care again and gave the heli my last two shots, not with any real hope; I don't know whether it was my slugs or Clark's that were responsible but there was a change in the note of the motor. It gave a high protesting whine as metal grated together and the big blades stopped chopping the air. I could see the heads of the pilot and

Hernando silhouetted against the clear dawn sky.

Then bright crimson flame grew like a rose from the body of the machine and enveloped it all; it fell with increasing velocity. The blades were turning now from the pressure of the air upon them; the machine hit the ground almost without sound and crumpled before spinning over into the ravine. The flame spread out like fluttering pennants and the whole thing went over into the tree-tops. A second or two later the thunder of the explosion reached us. I fell or was knocked down by the blast; tiny pieces of burning metal descended from the sky. I winced as one of them burned my cheek. None of them was bigger than a finger nail. I sat and looked at the oily smoke which ascended a hundred feet into the sky and waited for Clark to come up.

★　★　★

Macklehenny was still alive when we got back to the ambulance. Clark lifted him out tenderly from the back of the ruined machine. It was a real battle-painting in here, with bullet holes pocking the planking among the blood and twisted limbs. Macklehenny groaned once or twice as we set him down. Clark propped him against the side of the ambulance and felt among his clothing. He'd been shot twice in the gut.

'Take it easy, Charlie,' said Clark like he was talking to a child. It was only the second time I'd heard him use Macklehenny's Christian name.

'Sorry about that, Tom,' said Macklehenny, moving his eyes. Then he turned his head and died. A little pink froth formed and ran out of his lips. Clark got a handkerchief and wiped off the froth with great deliberation and put the handkerchief over Macklehenny's face. Then he sat down with his back to me and stared out across the field, saying nothing. I got up and searched about among the mess in the back of the ambulance.

The General's chair had turned over on its side and presented the splintered spokes of its wheels to my gaze. I crawled in and felt about under the blankets. The General lay on his side and the front of his jacket was a mess of scarlet. As he felt my fingers on his shoulder he slowly opened his eyes.

'Don't die, General,' I said. I figured I'd had about as much as I could take.

The General opened his eyes completely and the ghostly suspicion of a smile started gathering in the corners of his mouth.

'I have no intention of doing so, my dear sir,' he said, beginning to wipe the tomato ketchup off his shirt front. 'And if you will assist me out of this confounded thing I'll be much obliged to you.'

Clark got up quickly when he heard me shout; like me he took a bit of convincing. We got the General and the remains of his chair down out of the ambulance and set him up where he was looking at something peaceful. It was a bit difficult for whichever way you looked, it was like a slaughter house.

'I must confess I have a shrewd

suspicion of the feelings of Lazarus,' he said drily.

When Hernando had shot at him he'd pushed the chair over; the shot had smashed the partition of the driver's compartment. He'd already used the ketchup to make it look as though he'd been hit, for he knew they would come back to finish him if they couldn't get him off in the helicopter. Enterprise was always the General's trade mark. He'd heard all the shooting but had still played dead when we lifted Macklehenny out as he wasn't sure who had come back to the ambulance.

He sat up and looked at the sun which had come up over the edge of the trees. Clark fetched a blanket and covered Macklehenny over.

I felt drained of all life. I went and sat down. Then I put the Smith-Wesson on the grass and started to retch. I was still sitting there like a child when the field started to fill with cars. The place was full of big men in leather windcheaters; they had loud voices and rough hands and the kindest faces in the world. They brought hot coffee and whisky; they wore guns at their hips and State Trooper badges on their chests and they knew all about clearing up messes. I drank two cups of coffee and two slugs of whisky and then I couldn't take any more kindness and I passed out.

# 15

## Friendly Town

The last time I was in Mudville it was nearly Christmas and I had a few chores to do. The town looked about the same, no more no less than when I'd first set eyes on it. Yet there'd been so much mayhem the publicity had changed it in such a way that it would never be the same again. Not that I cared; it was one place I wouldn't be making a habit of.

I drove up to Patti Morgan's place; we'd met a couple of times in L.A. This time her people were at home. She introduced me. The father was a mild-faced, nice old guy with silver hair and tortoise-shell spectacles; the mother much younger and very sleek. I could see where Patti got her poise and grooming. They were pleasant people though and certainly knew how to make you feel at home. I left a small parcel when I came away.

'Not to be opened until Christmas,' I told her.

'I'll be seeing you before then,' she said with a smile. 'It's a secret.'

I shrugged. I went out to the car and came back with a package. It was a large cabinet portrait of Carmen Benson, blown up from the picture the Bensons had liked. Dame Dora had arranged it. I'd fixed it with Patti that she would take it along to the Bensons. Not at Christmas time, of course. Round about March, when the sting would have gone. We stood talking at the door. A young man arrived before I left. He gave me a suspicious look as he went by.

'Timber business?' I said.

She laughed. 'I'm a pretty practical girl. I figured the competition in L.A. was too stiff.'

She was talking about Stella. She brushed my cheek with her lips. 'See you, Mike,' she said and went indoors quickly.

I drove on down town. The weather was bitterly cold. It had been trying to snow all morning. Dame Dora's cheque rested snugly in my wallet. It burned a nice warm hole in the lining of my double-breasted.

Sheriff Clark was genuinely pleased to see me. 'Come on in, Mr Faraday.'

A plump-looking young man grinned and held out his hand to me. He sat at the other desk and pounded on his typewriter. Clark got out his old briar and stuffed it with tobacco. He fished up a bottle of bourbon from the recesses of his desk and poured generous shots for the three of us.

'Compliments of the season to you,' he said.

Presently we drove out to The Palisades. The lodge was still manned but the gates were wide open and there were no sentries. The General sat in a braided jacket and seemed very happy to see us. He insisted on serving the drinks himself. The short, broad-shouldered aide I'd seen before had been promoted to Rodriguez' place.

The General gave me a very handsome present before he left and wouldn't take no for an answer. He insisted on demonstrating his archery too. His aim and sight seemed as good as ever. When we went away at last it was already dusk. The housekeeper came running after us with a small brown paper package. When I opened it I found it contained my holster and the Smith-Wesson silencer. Clark grinned. He drove me downtown again.

'Who's your new assistant?' I said.

'Macklehenny,' he said. Seeing the surprise in my eyes, he went on, 'John Macklehenny, Charlie's boy. It runs in the family up here.'

I got in my car and sat with the engine idling. He put a strong hand in at the window for me to shake.

'So long, Mr Faraday,' he said. 'Any time you're up this way look us up. I shan't forget what you done.'

'Thanks, Tom,' I said.

He grinned and saluted. I gunned the motor and drove off quickly across town. Before I left I went into a booth and called Stella.

She sounded petulant. 'Do you know that tomorrow's Christmas Eve, Mike?' she said. 'We've got a million things to do and all the presents to get before we leave for mother's.'

'There's plenty of time, honey,' I said. 'I'm on my way in.'

Stella had persuaded me to go up and stay with her people this Christmas; it would make a nice change from my usual routine. I used to get in two extra bottles of Scotch and switch the TV on permanently. This Christmas looked like being a lot less painless.

'Dame Dora phoned,' said Stella. 'She wants us to go to her office Christmas party tomorrow afternoon. The two of you can do an exhibition judo bout.'

I groaned. That was Patti's surprise.

'Just so long as she doesn't want to play Postman's Knock,' I said.

After I came off the phone I got out of the drugstore. It was after six and quite dark. The shop windows looked kinda cosy in the gloom with their tinsel and coloured lights. The first thick flakes of snow were falling and from over the way came the faint notes of a youngsters' choir singing carols.

My last call was at Redbarn Autos for gas. Newton Cheney didn't seem to be doing so badly. He had a slightly built, grey-haired woman in the office with him whom he introduced as his mother. He didn't hold any grudges. He even shook hands when I came away.

'I took your advice, Mr Faraday,' he said.

'Like what?' I said.

'Like facing up to life. It worked out real fine. Do you think I'll make it?'

I gave him a long look, remembering a lot of things about Mudville and Carmen Benson.

'I think you'll make it,' I said.

I got in the Buick and drove out of town. On the way my headlights picked up something new. I got out of the car to see what it was. Though it wasn't really funny I couldn't help smiling all the way back to L.A. The Chamber of Commerce had taken my suggestion to heart after all.

They'd erected a big new, white-painted signboard at the edge of town. The wording, picked out in the simplicity of black paint merely said; WELCOME TO MUDVILLE. Population: 5,996.

THE BREAKING POINT
THE HOOK
PRINT-OUT
NIGHT FROST
THE LONELY PLACE
CRACK IN THE SIDEWALK
IMPACT
THE DARK MIRROR
NO LETTERS FROM THE GRAVE
THE MARBLE ORCHARD
A VOICE FROM THE DEAD
A QUIET ROOM IN HELL
HEAVY IRON
DEATH SQUAD
TURN DOWN AN EMPTY GLASS
THE CALIGARI COMPLEX
YOU ONLY DIE ONCE
HOUSE-DICK
SCRATCH ON THE DARK

We do hope that you have enjoyed reading this large print book.

Did you know that all of our titles are available for purchase?

We publish a wide range of high quality large print books including: **Romances, Mysteries, Classics, General Fiction, Non Fiction and Westerns.**

Special interest titles available in large print are: **The Little Oxford Dictionary Music Book, Song Book Hymn Book, Service Book**

Also available from us courtesy of Oxford University Press: **Young Readers' Dictionary (large print edition) Young Readers' Thesaurus (large print edition)**

For further information or a free brochure, please contact us at: **Ulverscroft Large Print Books Ltd., The Green, Bradgate Road, Anstey, Leicester, LE7 7FU, England. Tel:** (00 44) **0116 236 4325 Fax:** (00 44) **0116 234 0205**

*Other titles in the*
*Linford Mystery Library:*

# DEATH CALLED AT NIGHT

## R. A. Bennett

Jimmy Ellis believes his parents have died in a car crash when as a young boy he is taken to live with relatives in Australia. The years pass happily, then the nightmare comes. Terrifying images flit through his mind in the dark — all through the eyes of a child, a witness to grisly events seventeen years before. He begins to delve into the past, and soon he finds himself on the trail of a double murderer — a murderer who is prepared to kill again.

# THE DEAD TALE-TELLERS

## John Newton Chance

Jonathan Blake always kept appointments. He had kept many, in all sorts of places, at all sorts of times, but never one like that one he kept in the house in the woods in the fading light of an October day. It seemed a perfect, peaceful place to visit and perhaps take tea and muffins round the fire. But at this appointment his footsteps dragged, for he knew that inside the house the men with whom he had that date were already dead . . .

# THREE DAYS TO LIVE

## Robert Charles

Mike Harrigan was scar-faced, a drifter, and something of a woman-hater. With his partner Dan Barton he searched the upper reaches of the Rio Negro in the treacherous rain forests of Brazil, lured by a fortune in uncut emeralds. Behind them rode three killers who believed that they had already found the precious stones. And then fate handed Harrigan not emeralds, but the lives of women, three of them nuns, and trapped them all in a vast series of underground caverns.

# TURN DOWN AN EMPTY GLASS

## Basil Copper

L.A. private detective Mike Faraday is plunged into a bizarre web of Haitian voodoo and murder when the beautiful singer Jenny Lundquist comes to him in fear for her life. Staked out at the lonely Obelisk Point, Mike sees the sinister Legba, the voodoo god of the cross-roads, with his cane and straw sack. But Mike discovers that beneath the superstition and an apparently motiveless series of appalling crimes is an ingenious plot — with a multi-million dollar prize.

# THE DEAD DON'T SCREAM

## Leonard Gribble

Why had a woman screamed in Knightsbridge? Anthony Slade, the Yard's popular Commander of X2, sets out to investigate. Furthering the same end is Ken Surridge, a PR executive from a Northern consortium. Like Slade, Surridge wants to know why financier Shadwell Staines was shot and why a very scared girl appeared wearing a woollen housecoat. Before any facts can be discovered the girl takes off and Surridge gives chase, with Slade hot on his heels . . .